Forever 🌹 Romances

Imperfect Stranger

Carrole Lerner

Forever 🌹 *Romances*

is an imprint of
Guideposts Associates, Inc.
Carmel, NY 10512

Chapter One

It was a cool day for a Michigan August. Brianne Tyler pinned her latest safety cartoon on the Tech Center's announcement board and turned to go. She smiled at the sight of three tiny ducklings snuggled up to their mother outside, sunning their feathers with the rest of the ducks in this building's pond. Brianne wished she felt that peaceful.

Catching a strand of long dark hair that had escaped its gold clasp, she looped it behind her ear and returned to her office near the back of the Chevrolet building facing Van Dyke.

Her *temporary* office, she reminded herself. She'd been on this temporary service assignment at the auto company only six weeks, but she already felt at home. She typed for the sales and marketing representatives who had accepted her as one of their own, teasing her like a regular member of the crew. She would miss them when she moved on next week. *But!* she had to keep reminding herself, *it's only a job*, a means to an end, to make enough money to go on to grad school next year.

To do what? The uneasiness returned. She'd not given grad school much thought since she had met Spence.

She paused beside the long expanse of glass in the

lobby overlooking the retangular pool and fountains of the building's south entrance. Water from the fountain's jets danced blue-green in the sunlight before tumbling back into the pool.

Bree shivered in a draft from the air conditioner vent overhead. She hadn't heard from Spence since he'd left a week ago Saturday.

Spencer Kenyon. She'd grown more serious about him in the past four weeks than she realized. He knew it, too. And though he'd given her a 'commitment' ring set with a tiny opal she was still unsure of his true feelings for her.

Her commitment to Christ was a further barrier between them. He resented anything that took her attention away from him, scoffing at her involvement with church and friends till she let it slide to please him. That increased her uneasiness.

"*Nice* dress!" Dapper little Charlie Bates, one of the sales reps and a friend of Spence's broke into her distraction with an appreciative whistle. He held out a pack of gum, but she declined the offer. "You look like one of my wife's lon-n-ng-stemmed roses!"

Charlie commented on her height every time she wore heels to the office.

"Thanks," Bree said and flushed.

Charlie unwrapped his piece of gum, giving her an admiring nod. Bree knew the Polo shirt style of the designer dress complimented her slender figure, but she'd bought it more for the color. Dusty pink really set off her dark coloring, so the dress had been worth the rare splurge from her savings.

"I'm going to need every inch of my long stems to stand up to Neville Ross tonight!" She laughed and raised one foot to display three-inch heels on matching pink shoes.

" '*Digger*' Ross? The Aussie goalie who played with the Express a few seasons ago?" Charlie gave another low whistle. "The anniversary Manta's new pitch

6

person—" He shook his head speculatively. "I hear we were lucky to get him. His publisher added Detroit to his book tour at the last minute, and P.R. had to scramble to get him for their commercial."

"Go on, Charlie, tell me more!" Bree prompted with an impish grin. "Then I won't have to read that boring autobiography P.R. sent over!"

"Uh-uh. Do your homework," Charlie wagged a finger at her. "It's a cushy job—and read *Shootout*, too. It's pretty good." He started to add something but gave her an uncertain, sympathetic look, and changed his mind.

"It should be fun, Bree," he laughed instead and patted her arm, "Make the most of it!" With that he swung out the door to keep his afternoon appointment at a dealership.

Bree puzzled over the words and the look. Charlie had been at the convention with Spence last week. What did he know that she didn't?

Anyway, it hadn't occurred to her that serving as escort for Ross in his book and car promotions would be fun. It was glorified goferhood. P.R. tried to draft Maggie, her friend and supervisor who'd worked for McBain, but Bree volunteered in her place so panic-stricken Maggie could go on a family vacation. It would only be another week's work for Bree.

She swung down the narrow lane between the open area of the office where other stenos' desks were flanked by the glassed-in cubicles of managers' offices to her right. Her office fortunately had a good view of the whole area through the glass of the upper partition. It helped to be able to look up and see a little life and color outside her tiny cubicle—all beige, walls, furniture, even the Selectric.

Bree entered the office and smiled. The ball element of the old Selectric sat on the wood-topped metal desk where she'd left it. The multi-colored dahlias, blue cornflowers, and daisies she'd brought in that morning poked out of their green earthenware vase and made a welcome splash of color between the dull brown vinyl binders on the beige metal bookcase.

Shootout. What a strange title for an ex-soccer pro's autobiography, she thought.

"Maggie not here?" Gena Gibson lounged, one shoulder against the door frame. Her short-sleeved white linen suit and lime green blouse were dazzling against her newly acquired tan. The crispness of the fabric couldn't hide the type of figure Bree knew her brothers would describe as luscious.

"No, she's on vacation this week," Bree answered with indifference.

Gena, Spence's "main squeeze" pre-Bree. Spence assured Bree there'd been nothing between him and the secretary, but Gena's animosity followed Bree at work. He'd dismissed that with a laugh, but Bree could see he enjoyed it.

"What can I do for you, Gena?" Bree asked, trying to sound cordial but also to hurry Gena on her way.

There was a positive gloat in the sea-green eyes glittering down at her.

"Just thought I'd see if you need anything from the supply cabinet," she murmured and sauntered into the office to stare at the poster taped to the glass partition on Bree's left. "That's one fantastic car, Spence says...."

Bree gave her a sharp look.

Only the outline of the low, sleek sports car was visible under the red satin drape in the picture. The "revolutionary new design" that would make the Manta's second twenty-five years more exciting than the first was under tight wraps till next week.

But that wasn't what Gena was here for. Where had she seen Spence, and *when*? Bree's stomach tightened with her earlier apprehension.

"Ah, no, I don't need anything just now. Thanks anyway—" She wanted to ask Gena about Spence, but insight told her this was just what the other woman wanted. She searched her mind for another subject. "Have you got that report for Mr. Haney? He was just down here asking—"

Gena turned on her, eyes flashing in resentment and challenge. "You really make it hard to be nice to you Bree. I've *tried*, but you seem to have a need to pull rank on me!" Gena turned and strode to the door. Bree opened her mouth to protest, but her antagonist continued, "Just remember, *I'll* still be here when you're gone next week. I may even have a few surprises for you and Maggie. My work hasn't been entirely unnoticed around here!"

"Gena you *know* you're one of Maggie's best stenos," Bree tried to placate her. "As for my pulling rank," she addressed the accusation with a smile, "what *rank* can a 'rent-a-clerk'—as you rightly call me—have?"

Gena ignored the statement and conciliatory tone. She glanced back over one shoulder, foot poised above the doorsill.

"It wouldn't do you any good now anyway," she said mysteriously. "If you don't need anything I have things to do!"

Bree, her mouth still open in astonishment, shook her head to clear it. She picked up the Selectric's typing element to assault it vigorously with a blue wad of type cleaner. At least there were *some* things she could leave in good order when this job ended.

Gena's words had hit her in a vulnerable spot—the uncertainties and suspicions built on Spence's silence of the past week.

"Drat!" The type cleaner flipped from Bree's fingers and skittered across the desk. She looked up to find it and spied Spence through the glass, coming across the office toward her. Her hand shook. He *was* back! Why hadn't he called?

Bree watched him stop at Gena's desk, his sleek

9

dark hair brushing Gena's fiery copper curls as he leaned over to speak to her. Bree's heart constricted with dread.

Then Gena reached over to cover Spence's hand with her own, squeezing it possessively. Bree looked away; she didn't need to see more.

Their fight the night before he left, the silence afterward, and Gena's intimations all fell together to confirm the uneasiness snowballing at the back of her heart. Her romance with Spence was ending, over before it really began.

"Darn," she ducked her head to unobtrusively blot sudden tears from her eyes without smearing her makeup. Desperate for a diversion, she looked up again: "Where are you, you grimy little—"

The lopsided wad of putty lay atop the photo clipped to Ross's press kit.

"Oh no!" Bree grabbed the inky wad and the photo, holding it up to inspect it for damage.

Neville Ross's visage, sun-streaked tow hair spilling over the forehead above blue eyes, grinned roguishly back at her over the scrawled inscription, "Cheers, Neville Ross." At least she thought the eyes were blue. It was hard to tell from a black and white glossy.

"It's a good thing you didn't damage it, you nasty little dirt ball!" Bree told the type cleaner, jerking open her desk drawer to toss it in. Spence's ring rolled forward from the back where she'd hidden it. Bree felt a pang of guilt.

"And *you* stay there till I can get you bumped out, or however one gets a ring undented," she warned the small gold circle and slammed the drawer.

"Mind if I come in?"

Spence's voice was low and smooth as he stuck his head around the door. He gave her his most dazzling sales rep's grin, making Bree's heart pound in frantic foreboding.

A desperate prayer sprang to mind. *This is a fine*

time to get religion, Tyler! she chided herself, but she needed help. *Please, Lord, give me presence of mind and grace!* she breathed a silent appeal while her heart shriveled. *And if You would, Lord, don't let me make a bigger fool of myself by crying in front of Spence.*

It wasn't much of a prayer, but it brought her panic under control. She could face the situation now and sort it out later. At least she knew what Spence was up to.

"You know you're always welcome," Bree heard herself say cheerfully, tearing her eyes from his too-handsome face. "Did you have a good trip, meet lots of important people?"

"Yeah," he half laughed as he ambled to her desk stuffing his hands in the pockets of his charcoal colored suit.

Funny. She never noticed before, but no matter how hard Spence tried to dress the part of the conservative businessman, his own natural flamboyance always seeped through the facade. His electric blue shirt, though it intensified the color of his eyes—his chief vanity—jarred with the rest of his appearance and the image he tried to present.

He slouched forward, contracting his almost six-foot-tall frame.

"It was a great trip—fantastic!" He spoke with enthusiasm, running a careful hand over precisely styled hair. "Really good exposure for me." He glanced toward the outer office catching Gena's eye as she watched covertly from her desk.

What gall! Bree thought.

Spence's hands came out of his pockets to fidget with the card file on Bree's desk. He avoided her eyes.

"Gena was a great help!" His momentary distraction flared to enthusiasm again.

So *that's* where she was last week when everyone thought she was on vacation. Bree's faint hopes that she was misreading the whole situation began to sink.

11

"She knew all the right people to meet, McBain and the others," he continued. "I think I made a good impression on McBain—Now I really have a chance to get somewhere in this company, thanks to Gena."

"How very generous of her," Bree commented dryly. "I wasn't aware she'd gone to the convention." Even with outside help this conversation was getting hard to take.

"Yeah," Spence gave a nervous laugh. "The boss requested her, so she cancelled her vacation at the last minute and went. We had a *great* time!"

"What loyalty!" Bree bit out. Beneath the ebb and flow of conflicting emotions, a sense of calm asserted itself, carrying her along so that she felt she watched herself go through the motions from an outside vantage point.

But these paeans of praise to her successful rival grated. The heated looks that passed between Gena and Spence dispatched the last shred of hope she'd nurtured for him. She ran a piece of paper into the typewriter and snapped the bail down loudly.

"Ah…Bree, about last weekend…" Spence began, remembering the reason for this visit. He wandered to the bookcase below the poster to flip one of the fat brown binders on its spine and flick the colored divider tabs with a finger.

"…about last weekend," he began again. He saw she didn't intend to help him. He turned to her, twisting his chiseled, classic features into his most charming "pained" expression. "There's something I have to say, and it's not going to be easy for either of us—"

The words flowing from Bree's fingers onto the paper wavered before her eyes in a mist of unshed tears.

I thought you loved me, Spence! How can you do this to me?

All her anxieties of the past week rolled together into one great ball of anger. She wanted to scream, to accuse Spence of leading her on, but remembered words, learned long ago, floated to the top of her thoughts.

"Trust in the Lord with all thine heart...." She let go of the anger and felt it dissolve. There was nothing she could do to stop what was happening, but she could accept it. She felt then as if someone else guided her actions as she shuffled the notes she was typing and sped them onto the paper.

"Bree, I have something important to say—" Spence leaned across the desk, his fingers thrumming an impatient tattoo on its surface. "Can you stop that for a minute?"

"Oh. Sorry. This was a rush, and I thought I could rip it off while we chatted."

"Chat!" Spence exploded. "Is this what you think this is—a *chat?*" His voice crackled with irritation.

He paced agitatedly in the narrow confines of the cubicle.

"Well, for heaven's sake, what is it then?" Bree turned surprised eyes on him. She could accept what was happening, but she stubbornly refused to make the breakup easier for him. Especially not with Gena watching.

"Let's leave religion out of this for once, okay?" he snapped. Then he blurted, "I came in here to break up with you!"

By the startled way he looked around to see if anyone else had heard, it wasn't the way he planned to say it.

Bree looked at him, mildly surprised, and relaxed back into her chair.

"Is *that* all?" she chuckled softly, amazed to hear herself speak words at total variance with her true feelings. "You know, I'm relieved to hear you say that."

It would have been worse to hear it second hand, she thought.

"Bree," Spence enunciated his words carefully, suspicion flickering in his eyes, "did you hear what I said?

I'm *breaking up* with you!"

"No, Spence," she contradicted quickly, "*we* are breaking up with each other. It's much nicer that way, don't you agree?"

Of course he didn't. Spence was the dumper in his relationships, not the dumpee. A turnabout or even mutual agreement was incomprehensible to him.

"Breaking up *is* a good idea." She gave him that much, anyway. "I think we were too hasty about getting together in the first place."

He looked stunned. She reached over the typewriter to give his hand a comforting pat.

"I hope it won't hurt your feelings. I'll miss you," she said, allowing a slight wistfulness in her tone, "and I hope we can still be friends—but I just don't think we were right for each other."

Spence opened his mouth to speak, closed it, opened it again.

He noticed her hand as she withdrew it from his. "Where's my ring?" he demanded, alarmed. "It set me back a bundle. I hope you didn't lose it!"

"Oh!" she blinked. "The ring! I suppose the appropriate thing is to return it, right?" She'd truly forgotten it for the moment.

Bree opened the desk drawer, to the rattling accompaniment of loose change and other articles rolling around, and rummaged. "Here it is, little rascal!" She crowed triumphantly. "It rolled under the pencil tray!"

She held it out to him, steadying her hand by force of will when his hand brushed hers.

He gave her a dubious look and fingered the ring in his hand. "*You bent the band!*"

"Shhh! No need to yell!" she hushed him. "I *am* sorry about that. It got caught in the garbage disposal. Let me know when you have it repaired, and I'll gladly pay for it."

"Never mind!" he growled, pocketing the ring. His

self-assurance faltered visibly. He followed her gaze to the corner of her desk. "What are *you* staring at?"

Brianne picked up the glossy image of Neville Ross from the P.R. kit, letting her eyes run down it slowly.

"He's not bad looking for an ex-soccer pro," she mused, turning the photo around for Spence's inspection.

He snorted with disgust. "I thought you had better things to do around here than moon over jocks!"

"Spence! Keep your voice down!" she reminded with a glance at Gena's puzzled frown. Things didn't appear to be going as she expected.

"Besides, he's business," Bree continued. "I *have* to know what he looks like if I'm going to pick him up at Metro tonight."

Spence was unpleasantly surprised.

"*You!* Gena said they drafted Maggie for that job."

"P.R.'s timing was off. Maggie's gone on vacation, so Mr. McBain will have to settle for your friendly local temporary—me," she pointed out to his uncomprehending stare, "instead. It's cheaper than an outside escort service, and the star," she said, flicking a hand at Ross's photo, "specified *no* limos. So, I'll be his escort driver in a company car."

"*Lucky* Maggie!" Spence said viciously.

"Yeah," Bree sighed, hoping the Lord would forgive her just a touch of malice as she read aloud statistics from the star's bio: "Guess I'm stuck with this six-foot-four, two-hundred pound, blue-eyed, blond hunk for the whole week."

"A whole *week* with a big dumb jock!" Spence snarled and resumed his pacing, hands on hips.

"Don't be nasty," Bree defended her future charge. "He may not be dumb!"

"Sure! Sure!" Spence quit the field, his ego temporarily wounded. "Just don't come moaning to me next Monday about having to fend off this Neanderthal all week!"

He stamped to the door and was about to slam out.

"But Spence," Bree called softly after him, "why would I do that?"

He turned to scowl at her.

"We just broke up, remember?" she said.

Chapter Two

It had been a rough two hours since the incident with Spence. Brianne let the apartment door close behind her and leaned back against it. The effort to pretend nothing had happened—to suppress the hurt—took a lot out of her, but it worked. No one looked at her with pity, only curiosity because of the way Spence stalked out of the office and was a bear for the rest of the afternoon. She knew she owed the Lord a debt of gratitude for that.

But now the ache of the breakup hurt all over, like the pain two days after a hard physical workout.

Without thinking Bree picked up the mail lying on the foyer floor and stumbled down the hall to the living room, depositing it on a table. Her heart was a sodden lump in the center of her chest. Not even her drawing board by the dining el window or the easel in the corner with its half-finished oil of her cousing Karen tempted her to stop and daub, to lose herself in creating as she usually did when her emotions ran amuck.

Neville Ross! Neville Ross! The name ran through her head like a persistent drum beat moving her feet back through the cheery kitchen and down the hall toward the bathroom. There was no time to have a good cry or get down to business and pray about the hurt.

She had to get ready to meet Ross at Metro and start him on the round of promotional activities.

Blast Neville Ross! What a dumb time for him to come to town, she thought with resentment as she opened the linen closet at the end of the hall. She grabbed one of the big sea-mist green towels and slammed the white louvered door shut again. A tiny chip of paint popped off the edge in protest.

In the bathroom she found a note from Karen taped to the mirror.

"Gone to L.A.—back later in the week. Water Herbie!"

Karen, a flight attendant, spent more time away from her apartment than at home and had been glad to have Brianne move in with her when she returned from college. Brianne was just as glad to be on her own.

"Pick up Neville Ross, and water Herbie the fern," Bree mumbled making a mental list of her chores. She undressed, and set out her toiletries. She avoided looking at herself in the long mirror that took up one side of the bathroom above the sink and counter. With a bare foot she nudged the strawberry-pink-cushioned vanity bench under the counter out of her way.

Mechanically she turned on the water in the shower, adjusting the temperature. But with the rhythmic beating of the spray against the tub came the storm of tears she'd suppressed all afternoon. Bree sat down on the edge of the tub, propped her elbows on her knees, and sobbed all the pent-up hurt and disappointment into her towel. Long years of habit turned her mind to the companion who shared all her thoughts and hopes, to whom she'd looked for guidance till Spence came between them four weeks ago.

"I know it was my fault," she acknowledged, her mind dredging up events from the recent past. "You tried to warn me but I wouldn't listen. You showed me how egotistical and self-centered he was, but I didn't want to believe it. I thought he would change, would come to know You too, and would love both of us...."

Her mind rambled. The fact that she'd held Spence off physically so long almost convinced her he was becoming serious about her. But he had continued to make fun of her belief and commitment to God.

"Why mess with success?" he'd tell her with a crooked grin when she tried to talk with him about his own relationship with God. "I'm doing okay *without* divine interference."

"Be ye not equally yoked with unbelievers...." The words floated behind the lids of her closed eyes. Why hadn't she seen it sooner? Paul's words to the Corinthian believers haunted her. Hoping he'd come around, she'd let her own commitments slide for Spence, but that didn't work. She was always the one who wound up compromising, and the load of guilt had become unbearable. Last weekend was the final straw.

Bree burned with shame remembering the scene in the apartment after Spence gave her the opal ring and told her his hopes for their relationship. He expected a lot. She really had to fight her own emotions to hold him off then, to stop him from hustling her off to the bedroom to "seal their love" that night.

Her refusal made him angrier than she'd ever seen him. He left without saying good-bye or asking her to drive him to the airport. All he said was "I'll call you." It wasn't the way she had wanted their last evening before the convention to end.

She sighed into the towel. *It's all for the best*. The words ran like a song through her head. Mentally she believed it, but she knew it would take her heart a while to come around.

At last she was cried out and prayed out. On the heels of peace came a vehement resolve. She spoke it aloud as much in warning as to finalize it.

"One thing I promise You," she said, mopping her

19

face with the soggy towel, "I'll never again get involved with a man who doesn't share my trust in You."

The sound of her hot shower rushing down the drain brought Bree back to the present; she shot a panicked glance at her watch on the vanity.

"Look at the time! Now I've really got to move it to get to Metro!" She dived into the steaming jets to ready herself for the meeting with Ross.

There was one spot left in the short-term lot at Metropolitan Airport. Brianne aimed the company's metallic blue Camaro into it and braked with a screech of tires, jerking the key from the ignition.

Just ten minutes till Ross's flight was due to land she still had to check at the desk for the arrival gate number.

She practically ran through the lobby, slowing only to read the arrival-departure screen above the airline counter, and reached the gate with two minutes to spare.

Bree positioned herself at a post facing the ramp door and gave her reflection in the window a final check. The russet silk blouse with pussy-cat bow emphasized the brown flecks in her hazel green eyes and made a nice contrast with the raw silk suit—a graduation present from her brothers. The Chanel jacket of the suit, though less formal than the tailored gray she decided against, seemed more suitable to the occasion. Russet leather shoes and bag completed the outfit. Ordinarily she would have opted for lower heels than spikes, but she felt the added height might come in handy when she faced Ross's intimidating six-foot-four. She hoped he wasn't discerning enough to notice her almost total lack of makeup. She'd only had time for a dash of moss-green shadow, liner, bronze blusher, and a flick of red lip gloss. Her fine chestnut hair, drawn up into a loose knot atop her head was still uncomfortably damp, but it would have to do.

Brianne drew a breath to compose herself and took

Ross's photo from the P.R. kit.

"*Shootout*," she mumbled, "Why the strange title for an autobiography of a soccer player?"

She hoped he hadn't changed much since the photo was taken. There was no date to indicate how old it was though his age was listed as thirty-two.

"Thirty-two—" That seemed rather young to be retiring. Still, it was wise of him to do it while he could still enjoy the profits of his fame. Why did he retire? Bree remembered something about the event in the local papers last year, but the details escaped her. As she started to flip to the P.R. bio, the jumbo jet taxied by and nosed its way to the ramp outside. An attendant swung open the door and unhooked the chain across the entrance, and the crowd in the waiting lounge surged forward. After a few moments the first of the passengers deplaned. Happy cries, hugging, and excited voices babbling in unison greeted friends and relatives as the two groups mingled, broke off into smaller groups, and moved off down the corridor.

Brianne's stomach churned with sudden nervousness. She practiced her little speech, hoping she would sound more businesslike than she felt. For a split second she wished she'd never volunteered for the job. What did she know about escorting celebrities anyway? Just then she saw Ross—he would have been hard to miss.

His head just seemed to clear the top of the door as he entered the waiting room and glanced around. Brianne took the opportunity to appraise him.

He dominated the lounge by sheer physical presence. A magnificent specimen of athletic power and grace, he moved toward Bree. Her artist's eye compared him to da Vinci's and Michelangelo's anatomical sketches. The way his kelly green Ralph Lauren knit shirt molded to a perfectly proportioned chest and wide shoulders, he was an ad for the designer. White linen slacks emphasized the length of his legs and matched the jacket tied carelessly around his neck. One hand held a flight bag, while the other slung a suitbag behind him.

To Bree's amazement he spotted her instantly and made straight to where she stood, his chin jutting forward determinedly. Then even, white teeth flashed as he grinned, a startling contrast against the golden tan of his skin. And his eyes—his eyes were indeed blue. British blue, she tagged it, that intense brilliant cerulean of October morning skies.

"Neville Ross!" He introduced himself without preamble, shifting the suitbag to hold out one large hand. He breathed a fervent sigh and laughed. "Thank God you're pretty! Don't think I could take another week in the company of an escort like I had in Chicago—three hundred pounds if he weighed an ounce and looked like he could go fifteen rounds with a champion heavyweight!"

His easy charm made it hard not to like him. Bree was forcefully reminded of her brother's overly sociable golden retriever!

"Sorry! Here I am running off at the mouth without giving you a chance to introduce yourself!—You *are* my escort?" A worry line of doubt flickered across his brow.

"Brianne Tyler," she confirmed with a tight smile thinking, *Better get things back in control here Tyler. You're supposed to be running this show.* "Let me take that bag for you."

Without waiting for a reply she lifted the heavy flight bag from his shoulder, and almost staggering under its weight, she managed to sling it over her own. She wondered what in the *world* he had in it.

"The claim area is this way, down the escalator," she continued. "They'll probably have the rest of your luggage unloaded by the time we get there."

"It's been a while since I've been here but I think I know the way," he said, bewildered by her aloofness, his voice echoing the puzzled look he gave her.

Bree felt a twinge of conscience about that. Business *is* business she told herself, and she intended to finish her last week with the company as efficiently as possible.

It took some doing, but Bree led the way down the corridor. She had to take two steps to every one of his to stay ahead of him.

"My but we're in a hurry!" Neville observed wryly behind her.

"You have a very full schedule," Bree told him over her shoulder. She took a stapled itinerary from the folder under her arm to pass back to him. "Soon as you've freshened up and changed, I'll take you to dinner. There's an excellent restaurant in your hotel. Then you're scheduled for a reception at Mr. McBain's for dessert and coffee."

She heard pages rustle as Ross scanned the schedule.

"They certainly plan to get their money's worth out of me," he said with a low whistle. "Looks like I won't have a minute to myself."

"I'm sure it won't be that bad." Conscience-stricken, Bree turned to assure him. He reached forward and grabbed her elbow, bringing them both to a halt.

"I'd prefer to talk *to you*, not *at* you back," he said softly, holding her down to a walk beside him as they moved forward again. "And if you're going to be my pilot through the treacherous shoals of book parties, talk shows, casting meetings, and commercial filmings, the pleasure of your company will make up for this flurry of activity. That is, if you can see your way clear to relax a little."

He grinned coaxingly and stopped again, swinging her around to face him. With one finger he tipped her chin up to look into her eyes. The blueness of his eyes reminded her of Spence, and *his* determined pursuit of her those first few weeks at work before she finally let her guard down.

She drew a shaky breath. It was unfair to compare the two. Spence's line had been smooth, calculating, unlike Neville Ross's natural directness. It was unfair of her to take out the anger and frustration over her broken romance on Ross. She was surprised to see concern in his eyes as they probed hers.

"Cheer up," he encouraged, mistaking the direction of her thoughts. "Are you having second thoughts about escorting me already? Remember you're the one who said it wouldn't be so bad."

"I'm sorry—please forgive me." She owed him an apology of sorts. "I've had a rough day, but that's no reason to take it out on you."

His smile, crinkling the corners of his eyes, had a soothing effect. He caressed her chin with the tip of his finger and sighed.

"I'll have to remember that apology," he mused. "I may have to repeat it to *you* before this week is out. Now! Shall we go collect my worldly goods? I'm looking forward to that dinner you promised. You're sure that bag of books isn't too heavy for you—?"

Chapter Three

At the Troy Hotel Brianne declined Neville's invitation to wait for him in his room, even though it was a suite with adjoining sitting room. She felt uncomfortable going to a man's room alone, and he didn't press the issue. But he might have, she thought, if she'd told him she'd grown up with four brothers!

"What d'you think? Will I pass inspection?" Neville appeared before her as she pored over the schedule in the lobby.

Though he'd showered and changed, his appearance was still more California casual than dress-for-success. He'd changed the green shirt for navy and wore gray flannel slacks and a navy blazer with heraldic design on the breast pocket. Bree was reminded of her first impression of him at Metro—that he'd make a terrific shirt model. Black slip-ons with a gold ornament replaced the boater moccasins and were his only concession to formality.

He noted her questioning look.

"We celebrities are allowed a bit more eccentricity than you workaday types," he grinned. "Now where's this restaurant? I'm starved!"

"This way!" Brianne rose and led the way across the lobby, hurrying to open the door for him. She ignored his startled look. "Hope you like seafood. This is one of the best places in town for it."

They nearly wrestled over the chair when she started to pull it out to seat him. He took her arm firmly in hand and led her around to the other side of the table before seating himself. But after first consulting him, she did order for them.

While he made short work of scallop appetizers and then an entrée of steak and two lobster tails, she picked at her seafood salad, trying to guide conversation about the week's schedule. "You have an early morning talk show appearance tomorrow. Then it's on to Dayton's for an author's tea and autograph party at noon," she pointed out. "In the afternoon, P.R. has set up the shooting schedule for the Manta commercials."

The atmosphere was much too intimate to concentrate on the business at hand. Brianne had to squint at the schedule in the low light of the elegant hurricane lamp on the table. Neville was studying her throughout the meal with politely restrained but mounting curiosity. Polite restraint lost out. He laid down his fork, fixing his eyes on her.

"Brianne, I don't really know you well enough to be saying this, I know, but I'm hazarding a guess that something that happened today has you turned around." He placed one hand over hers on the table. "If there's anything I can do—I don't mean to pry, of course. I know I'm a perfect stranger...."

"*Nobody's* perfect," Bree said politely. She pulled her hand away, dropping her gaze from his acute scrutiny. It embarrassed her that her feelings were so obvious. But there was no way she could tell him about this afternoon and Spence. She would have to be more careful. The man was entirely too perceptive.

"...an *imperfect* stranger then," he amended. "We're going to be spending a lot of time together this week, and I'd like it to be as pleasant as possible for both of us. I don't like to see people unhappy...." He grinned at her. "Especially pretty ones. I am a good lis-

26

tener, and these shoulders can do more than block soccer balls. Remember that."

"Thanks," she said looking up again. "I'll keep that in mind." She hastened to change the subject. "Tell me about Mr. McBain."

"Oh, Mickey!" He laughed and launched into an explanation that carried them through the rest of the meal and on to the reception.

Rob Roy McBain, head of Public Relations, had been a "mate" of Neville's father when he'd worked at the Tech years ago. They were leaders of the team that came up with the original Manta sports car twenty-five years ago. Neville was in town to promote the faster, sleeker anniversary version.

"Mickey's known me since I was barely able to stumble over a soccer ball—we call them footballs on the other side of the pond, you know!" he informed Brianne. McBain kept in touch with the Rosses when Neville's dad transferred back to the Australian division of the company. When Neville played a couple of seasons with the Express, Mickey was his biggest fan and booster. He was at the championship game that ended Neville's career in pro soccer and was the first to offer him a place in the company if he wanted it.

The last two items were news to Brianne. What could an ex-soccer pro possibly do in an auto company? Before she could ask, he pointed out the drive of McBain's home, and she turned in, following the long, curving route toward an Italianate gray stone mansion, its long piazza semi-hidden in formally landscaped grounds. Poplars like tall columns of green smoke lined the drive. Topiary punctuated the arched windows opening onto the piazza, and figures shifting in conversational groups were silhouetted against the filmy curtains billowing in the faint breeze.

Brianne parked the car in the drive and they mounted the low, deep steps flanked by banks of scarlet geraniums. She inhaled their earthy green scent, preparing for her first foray as a celebrity escort.

A liveried butler ushered them into the foyer, his face lighting in recognition of Neville.

"A pleasure to see you again, sir," he murmured.

"It's good to be back home again, Parker," Neville said warmly. The butler smiled widely as he returned to his post at the door.

Brianne spotted Robby McBain as soon as they entered. He held court in the midst of a group of executives, entertaining them with highlights of his adventures with the company. He was a slight man of medium height with salt-and-pepper hair, and his gray eyes sparkled with laughter as he spoke. His expensively tailored gray suit spoke of an innate good taste.

"Neville!" He suddenly spied Neville and Brianne and hurried to greet them. His affection for the tall Australian was evident as he grabbed his hand, pumping it vigorously before clapping him on the back. "It's good to see you navigating on your own two feet again, my boy!"

"Indeed, Mickey," Neville agreed. His hand enveloped that of his host. "They put me back together well enough," Neville replied quickly, giving Brianne the impression he did it to forestall questions about the injury. She was curious about it now.

"See?" He held out his right leg, flexing it. She could see the outline of what looked like an athletic knee brace through the fabric of his trousers.

"Well enough to give the new Manta Silver Smoke Edition a test spin tomorrow?" McBain asked with a sly wink. His eyes twinkled a challenge. "And I may have a little surprise for you Friday as well."

He noticed Brianne at Neville's side.

"Well, who have we here?" His eyebrows rose in interest and admiration.

"Brianne Tyler, Mr. Ross's escort for the week," she introduced herself.

"Tyler, Tyler—where have I seen that name recently? The cartoons—you drew the cartoons on the bulletin board!" he said, pleased with himself for making the connection. "Very good, too! I've instructed my secretary to contact you about using them in the house paper."

Bree flushed with pleasure. It wasn't often her art attracted notice from someone able to publish it. She'd never had any formal art training, though she would have liked to.

"You're an artist?" Neville looked at her with new interest. "I'd like to see some of your work."

"If we have time," she replied. "I believe Mr. McBain is waiting for you so he can begin the meeting!"

"Everyone's been anxious to meet our newest endorser," McBain winked at Bree. "But they'll have to wait till I get through with him first! Why don't you introduce yourself to Mrs. McBain and have some refreshments while you're waiting, Miss Tyler?" He indicated a slender, elegantly dressed woman in a white crepe cocktail dress, "Nellie, oh Nell, can you come here a minute?"

She excused herself and smiled pleasantly as she made her way to her husband's side.

"Nell, this is a friend of our Neville's," McBain introduced Brianne, much to her embarrassment and Neville's unabashed delight. "Why don't you take her around and introduce her while we're busy in the study?"

After an enthusiastic hug from Eleanor McBain and before her husband dragged him off to a room at the other end of the long living room, Neville leaned down to whisper in Brianne's ear, "You're in *good* hands!" Bree caught glimpses of dark wood paneling and tall rows of bookshelves crammed with antique volumes before the study door closed behind the men.

"Well, I must say I approve," Nell cast a friendly glance over Brianne. "You're certainly one of the pret-

tiest of Neville's young friends we've met so far!"
Brianne thought Mrs. McBain herself quite lovely, with
a reserved hauteur belied by lively, dancing dark eyes.
She took Bree up to a group of women and introduced
her before moving on to continue her hostessing functions.

After exchanging pleasantries with the women,
acutely aware of their curious stares, Bree wandered
away on the pretext of admiring the rest of the room.
At a loss to occupy herself further, she realized she'd
better learn. She was going to spend a lot of time waiting
for Neville in the next few days.

There was enough to admire. The McBains were collectors of pre-Columbian art and she lingered over
primitive clay sculptures and other artifacts displayed
throughout the room.

She wandered the length of the room and out the
end doors through the solarium with its myriad hanging plants and potted palms, then back into the reception room again.

She spotted two tables set up before the tall windows overlooking the piazza.

Better act like I belong here, she told herself and
strolled over for a closer look.

A maid in a frilly cap and apron ladled punch into
crystal cups. An exotic array of hors d'oeuvres was arranged on silver chargers to either side of the huge
crystal punch bowl. Another maid poured coffee from
a silver coffee urn into delicate china cups. From miniature French pastries on china dessert plates, Bree
chose a chocolate éclair, nestled temptingly in a lace
paper doily. Thanking the maid for the coffee, she juggled the two plates to a secluded spot behind two
palms and sank into the orchid print overstuffed chair.

It felt good to slow down. She set the plates on a
glass-topped wrought iron table, beside a round clear
vase of lavender gladioli sprays and stirred the coffee
gently to cool it.

"Sitting down on the job already!"

Bree jumped, nearly spilling the coffee as Spence's cryptic voice cut her peace to ribbons.

"Um-hum!" To steady her hands she picked up the éclair and took a bite without looking up.

Casually she turned to face him, the panic of the afternoon knotting her stomach all the while. Gena stood beside him in a form-fitting, midnight-blue dinner dress, one hand looped possessively through his arm. Her sea-green eyes jealously took in Brianne's raw silk.

"I guess you're wondering why I'm here," Spence said, Bree's steady regard putting him on the defensive.

"Well, since you're not exactly a close friend of Mr. McBain yet, the thought *did* cross my mind!" She smiled pleasantly *Oh, Lord,* she prayed, *watch over me and guard my tongue. Don't let me be a reproach to You.* She felt again the peace of commitment to her Lord dispelling the anxiety of facing Spence.

"Gena was invited—I told you she went to the convention, didn't I? Well, McBain remembered she was a fan of Ross's when he played for the Express and invited her to meet him tonight." Spence made a point of looking into Gena's eyes and squeezing her hand.

Bree averted her eyes. Taking up her spoon she gave the coffee a couple more swirls. "Why is it they always make the coffee too hot to drink?" she asked of no one in particular. Her chest constricted. It hurt to see them together. Why didn't he just go away and leave her alone? Did he take some sadistic pleasure in taunting her this way? No—she'd injured his pride by breaking up first this afternoon, so he had to retaliate.

"Well, Gena, since you're so anxious to meet Neville—" Brianne started to speak.

"*Neville!* Isn't it a little soon to be on a first-name basis?" Spence interrupted.

"I'll be sure to introduce you myself," Bree finished

31

and gave Gena a bright smile.

"Very big of you," Spence growled. "Bree, you're the last person I would have expected to have your head turned by all this," he chastised her. "Only one hour in the company of the rich and famous and you're already putting on airs!"

"Airs?" Bree gave him a hurt look. "Neville and I will be spending a lot of time together this week since I'm responsible for getting him to his appointments. And, by the way, Spence," she dropped her voice conspiratorially and gave him a wink, "be careful not to let Neville steal Gena from you. He's an *outrageous* flirt, a very charming man!"

Neither Spence nor Gena liked that, and it was small comfort to Brianne. With the draining effort to keep up her charade of indifference to Spence, she felt as if she'd run a marathon.

"Thanks for the offer, but I think we'll manage without your help," Spence said. He started to move away with Gena.

"Leaving so soon?" Neville's voice spoke from behind Bree. He sidestepped the palm to stand beside her, flipping a radish rose up and down in his hand. "Introduce me to your friends, my dear." He touched Brianne's shoulder lightly with his hand. Spence frowned.

"Neville Ross, Spencer Kenyon and Gena Gibson." Bree performed the duty with businesslike directness. Neville sized up and dismissed Spence with a cursory glance and turned to Gena. "Gena is one of Mr. Mc-Bain's secretaries, and a fan of yours from Express days." Bree added the last as an afterthought, realizing how catty it sounded only when Gena flashed her an angry look. Well, it was nothing more than Gena was going to say herself. To Bree's amusement, Gena, an accomplished flirt, let go of Spence's arm to glide forward sensuously and take Neville's hand in both her own.

" 'Digger' Ross!" she breathed huskily. "I've wanted to meet you for *years!* I went to every home game the Express played when you were on the team—and I think you're the greatest player they ever had!"

"Thank you." Neville beamed at her, but withdrew his hand from her grasp after giving her hands a quick squeeze. "That's very kind and very flattering. If you're one of Mickey's secretaries I'll probably be seeing a lot of you in the next week. Have you been to the hors d'oeuvres table yet? Eleanor McBain's are noted for exotic variety, you know." He dropped down on the arm of Bree's chair leaning one arm across behind her to balance himself. "Brianne, my dear, help me 'do the pretty' and meet all these people!" He turned a look of mock appeal on Bree. There was a wicked gleam in his laughing eyes as he leaned closer to her.

Feeling through her pain the strong pull of Neville's personal magnetism, Bree found it hard to resist resting her head against the shoulder so near her.

But taking his cue she said, "Certainly. I'm sure Spence and Gena will excuse us."

Neville stood with easy grace and pulled Bree to her feet. He kept her hand in his to hold her beside him. Spence's eyes burned into her as he took Gena's hand and drew it through his arm again.

"Nice meeting you, Kenyon," Neville said. The two men shook hands—Spence warily, Neville with polite dismissal. He popped the radish into his mouth and bit it with a loud crunch.

"You'll see more of me during the week, Ross," Spence said baring his teeth in a cold smile. It suddenly struck Brianne why he was being surly. He was *jealous*—not of Neville's flirting with Gena, but of his attentions to herself. His next words confirmed it. "Brianne and I are friends, you know."

Gena gave him a murderous look.

"Let's go find Mr. McBain. I'm sure he's got some interesting people for you to meet," she purred, drawing Spence away.

"He's not *really* a friend of yours, is he?" Neville turned to regard her with an incredulous stare when they were out of earshot.

"Not anymore," Bree said dryly.

"Glad to hear it!" He spoke in a low rumble. "I gave you credit for more discernment in your choice of friends. He's a bit on the flashy side—*pushy,* too!" He surprised her again. "Care to talk about it?"

She didn't know if he'd come to her rescue or his being in that particular spot was a lucky coincidence. Was he putting the pieces together—her behavior that evening and the scene between her and Spence just now? She wanted to trust him, but she still couldn't talk about it. No matter how comfortable she felt with Neville Ross, he was still a stranger, an outrageous flirt, and much too attractive!

"No, I'd rather not," she finally answered. *He's business, Tyler!* she further admonished herself. *He'll be gone at the end of the week and so will this assignment.*

He accepted her refusal and let the subject drop. "Shall we make the rounds then?" he said and started toward a group of executives and their wives who looked his way expectantly. One or two of the women stared pointedly at Bree's hand, still clasped in Neville's. She withdrew it and stepped back from the circle that quickly formed around him.

As he answered a barrage of questions about himself and his plans a thought that had been nibbling at the back of Bree's consciousness burst through: on the *other* hand why *not* make the most of the situation handed to her? Flirt back with the man—enjoy his attentions to her. Neville was obviously willing. She could throw herself into the job of escorting Neville, concentrate entirely on him. It would help her forget Spence. There was no chance she could get romantically involved with Neville. The fact that he was leaving at the end of the week, and most importantly, her promise to God earlier that day precluded that.

But then, she didn't really know what Neville believed, except that she was probably just another pleasant distraction on the promotional tour. It was a harmless game they could both play.

Neville was silent as she guided the car through the winding streets of West Bloomfield back to Woodward Avenue. Mentally reviewing her plans for him Bree felt uneasy and was grateful for the silence.

"Nell has invited us for brunch Sunday morning," he finally spoke. Shifting in the bucket seat of the Camaro he lay one arm across the top of her seat. The smallness of the car put him much too close. The faint spicy scent of his aftershave tantalized her.

"Us?" she questioned, happy for the darkness that hid her expression from his knowing eyes. She sensed rather than saw his slow grin. "We're not an 'us.' Surely she knew I'm just your escort."

"She thought we made a good couple," he chuckled, a deep, pleasant-sounding, throaty rumble. 'You're not going to disappoint her are you?"

This was moving too fast. Her "game" didn't include getting involved with Neville's friends.

"I don't think I should go. It would be passing myself off as something I'm not." A better reason to decline the invitation came to mind. "Besides, I go to church on Sunday mornings."

He nimbly cleared that hurdle.

"I'm sure Nell could make it a late luncheon in that case," he said.

"You're teasing me!" she accused. "She didn't really invite me at all."

"Of course I'm teasing you—you're eminently teasable—but she really *did* invite you." He lapsed into silence again for a moment. "Why don't you think about it?"

There wasn't any time to say more. She pulled into the lot of the hotel and found a spot. But as she reached for the door handle, his hand shot out and closed around hers, holding her captive in the circle of his arms.

"No, you don't," he breathed softly. His face was inches above hers. She could feel his breath, warm on her cheek. He smiled languidly and lowered his lashes, and for a moment she was afraid he was going to kiss her. "If you intend to 'nanny' me, Miss Tyler, I'd like to keep you alive long enough to finish the job. I don't want you returning to the car alone in the dark. Therefore you will *not* see me to my door."

He dropped a quick kiss on the tip of her nose and was out of the car door before she could protest. His laughing voice floated back to her on the cool night air:

"Good night, Nanny!"

Chapter Four

There was no Neville in the lobby the next morning when Brianne arrived, congratulating herself on being punctual. She checked her watch. They had forty-five minutes. Just enough time to get from Troy to the TV studio in downtown Detroit.

She wandered around the lobby glancing toward the elevator each time it discharged a load of passengers. Still no Neville.

Five minutes passed. Then ten.

"He knew what time we had to be there!" she fumed. "It's going to be tight as it is!"

She went to the desk, asked to use the phone, and dialed his number. The phone rang several times before he picked it up.

"Ross here."

"Yes, I know you're *there*, but you're supposed to be *here*," she greeted him. "Are you ready yet?"

A sigh, then a pause at the other end of the line.

"Come up and get me, copper!" he snarled. The line went dead as he hung up.

His voice was surly. What had happened to put him in a bad mood so early, Bree wondered. Hadn't he had breakfast yet?

Exasperated she stalked across the lobby to the elevator and jabbed the UP button. Then she halted uncertainly, memory of the unaccountable attraction she'd felt for him last night still fresh in her mind.

"Don't be ridiculous, Tyler," she chided herself. "It's business, remember, just part of the job. He was just being nice because he's glad you didn't turn out to be a sumo wrestler like the Chicago escort."

She reached his door with her confidence restored and knocked.

No answer. She knocked louder.

"Neville, are you in there?" she muttered. From the little she knew of him it wouldn't be out of character for him to make her come up to get him, then say, "What kept you?"

"I'm coming, I'm coming!" she heard his agitated baritone grumble from the other side of the door. He swung it open and motioned her in. "Be ready in a sec."

He was dressed in a navy blazer and gray slacks again, but he wore a blue shirt this morning with silver and blue striped tie. Apparently the tie had caused his ill humor. Bree watched him fumble with its knot before the bureau mirror.

"*Mind the glass!*" he cautioned as something crunched under her shoe. Shards of glass lay scattered on the carpet, radiating from a picture frame face down in the corner. A tiny nick in the wallpaper and the broken corner of the wooden frame told the story: he'd thrown it in a fit of pique. But at whom?

Bree bent to pick it up for him.

"*Leave it!*" he snapped. Then, "Sorry!—could you help me with this blasted collar button? I'll bend down."

"Not necessary," Bree said. "Having long arms is one of the advantages of being tall."

She was busy coaxing the stubborn button through the hole, but she felt his breath on her forehead and caught his wry smile from the corner of her eye. She stepped back self-consciously.

"*Now* are you ready, Mr. Ross?" she asked with a stern look to cover her confusion. He seemed more than willing to go along with the little game she had in mind.

"Yes, Nanny." He used the name he'd given her last night and gave her a contrite grin. "By the way, you look lovely. Red is certainly your color."

She acknowledged the compliment and turned away from his admiring appraisal to lead the way down the hall.

She'd worn a blue blazer herself, over her red print dress, and had combed her hair into a side part pulling it back with a gold clasp to let the rest fall free in a sable froth around her shoulders.

"Just a minute." He grabbed her elbow as she opened the car door for him and swung her around to face him. Not knowing what to expect, she flinched. "Turnabout's fair play."

He grinned and gave the red print bow at the neck of her dress a straightening tug.

At the studio she turned Neville over to an anxious producer and found a seat at the back of the small studio to watch.

The producer, a fair-haired young man in blue shirt, tan pants, and boaters came on to warm up the audience and instruct them how and when to applaud. The half hour till air time passed quickly while Bree surveyed the interior of the first TV studio she'd ever seen.

The seats were just metal chairs on the floor. It would have been hard to see over the heads of people in front of her. But being tall gave her an advantage.

The heat radiating from the banks of lights overhead made her want to shed her jacket, but intermittent blasts of cold air from the air conditioner convinced her to keep it on. What appeared on TV to be walls of

39

the studio were in fact gray curtains on either side of the audience.

Finally the host came out and everyone applauded and cheered enthusiastically. The show was under way. A comedian appearing at a local supper club and a plant psychologist who reminded Bree guiltily of Herbie preceded Neville, who was third on the guest list.

His easy charm won the audience immediately. Bree watched with a touch of proprietary pride as he chatted affably with the hosts about his soccer career and his book.

Then to her surprise they showed a clip of his last game as a professional player.

Bree watched with interest the monitor facing the audience as the film rolled. It was the last few minutes of the game. Neville scooped the ball down out of the air, but as he fell with it his right knee twisted under him. Two opposing players, unable to check their speed, tumbled on top of him and the audience groaned. His team won the championship on that save.

Some of his teammates did a victory dance around the field carrying their trophy, but a couple remained with Neville as medical attendants lifted him on a stretcher to carry him off the field and out of professional soccer.

Bree thought she caught a glimpse of what the incident had cost him in his anguished expression as he writhed on the stretcher clutching the injured knee. She felt a sense of loss for him, but Neville's expression as he reviewed it remained pensive.

"The end of one thing is often the beginning of another," the host commented turning to Neville as the film ended. "We know you're in town plugging your book, but aren't you also shooting commercials for the twenty-fifth anniversary of the Manta? Rumor has it you're going to be joining the company in another capacity as well."

Bree's ears perked up. The only thing she'd heard was Mickey's offer of a place in the company. Neville never mentioned a definite commitment. She felt excluded, as if he'd withheld information from her.

Whoa, girl! He doesn't owe you explanations for anything. You're just an escort, remember?

She sighed, *Right!* She couldn't afford to let his considerable charm get to her—not after what she'd been through with Spence. *Heaven help me to learn from that experience and remember my promise,* she breathed to herself. There was no telling what *this* man believed.

Neville's voice caught her attention again. He looked her way and cocked a brow quickly.

"Harry, I've found that nothing is ever certain in this life except the leaving of it," he laughed. "There's been a lot of talk, and I can't say what kind, but no definite answers yet. Sorry."

"Maybe you can answer some questions for our studio audience. Our call number is on the screen...."

"You handled it very well," Bree complimented him when it was over. "One would think you've been in show business instead of soccer."

"I *feel* like I have—been in show business," he ammended, running a hand through the carefully brushed thick hair. Bree thought it looked better for the rumpling. "This has been going on for three weeks."

He sounded tired and distracted. She shot him a glance of concern.

"You'll be glad when it's over, won't you?" she sympathized.

"Well, yes," he drawled, fixing her with a long look, "but I'm not looking forward to the end of *this* week."

"But after New York you'll be through," she reminded.

He rolled his eyes and gave her a crooked grin.

"This week will also be all there is for us." He cut off her protest. "I owe you an apology for being such a bear this morning."

"No problem," she assured him. Memory of the picture frame on the floor of his room popped into her mind. She asked mischievously, "Care to talk about it?"

He sighed, leaning his head back against the headrest.

"No. Not now. Suffice it to say Mickey told me what his 'surprise' was this morning. It was not—as he'd thought—a pleasant one for me."

His eyes darkened and his expression closed. This was a side of Neville Ross she hadn't seen before—the dark and secret side of an otherwise sunny personality.

Impulsively she reached over and took his hand. She wanted him to know she understood and respected his feelings. But when she tried to pull it away he gripped it tightly and raised it to his lips. The warmth of his mouth as he held it pressed to her fingers tingled up her arm.

Spence had never kissed her hand like that. He'd never kissed it at all. But why was she even thinking of Spence? There was just no comparison between the two men.

He caught and held her eyes with his gaze. Something crackled in the look that passed between them.

Afraid to speculate about it, she pulled her hand away. "I need both hands to navigate these interchanges," she explained.

He smiled slowly. "Have dinner with me tomorrow night," he said. He held up a hand to fend off her objections. "*No* arguments, and don't try to take charge. I'm pretty sure the schedule is open."

He whipped the folded schedule from between the pages of his book to consult.

"Yes, right here! I have a meeting with Mickey and the others. I'll have it moved up and give you time to go home and change, then come back for me."

"But I can't—" She was at a loss. "It wouldn't seem right. You didn't take the Chicago wrestler out to dinner did you?" Her objectivity was at stake.

"*Boxer*, dear, not wrestler," he corrected, chuckling. "And yes, I did take him to dinner. If it's your job you're worried about, don't. I'll square it with anyone who cares to take umbrage at mixing business with pleasure."

There was no time to argue. They'd arrived at the department store where the noon autograph party was being held and had to hurry to make it on time.

The rest of the afternoon passed in a flurry of activity that left Bree grateful as she dragged herself up the stairs to her apartment that evening. Neville was spoken for the rest of the evening, so she was free to try and unwind. She wondered how he'd put up with the staggering pace for three weeks. She was exhausted after just one day of it!

She chuckled to herself. He certainly had a knack for dealing with people, she mused, shuffling the mail.

After lunch a mob of mothers, assorted children and toddlers had descended on him. The women, who had children in local youth soccer leagues, came by to point him out to the youngsters for inspiration. Stopping to chat they wound up buying the book as well as flirting with the handsome ex-pro. He didn't bother to discourage them.

When younger siblings swarmed around him, some still clutching sticky candy treats from the store restaurant's kiddie special, he hauled them jovially into his lap to autograph the backs of their tee shirts. His patience seemed endless. Bree had stood back and looked on in admiration.

Kicking off her shoes she curled her aching toes in the carpet's thick pile. Evening sunshine poured in the multipaned bay window across the room to make a hopscotch board of light squares on the floor.

"Herbie!" she cried. Flinging the mail on the chair beside the window recess she hurried across the room to check the fern hanging in the corner. Dry as a bone.

Conscience stricken she rushed to the kitchen, filled the watering pot, and swung around, sloshing water on the floor in her haste to save the plant. The phone rang.

"Nuts!" she exclaimed, grabbing it off the wall with her free hand. "Hello!" she barked.

"Brianne Noel!" an equally reproachful voice replied. "*Where* have you been?"

"Jack!" Bree laughed helplessly, "I've been busy. Ferrying Neville Ross around to TV appearances and book-signing sessions is no picnic you know. Didn't Mom tell you?"

"No kidding!" her brother exploded. "You don't mean that big goalie who played for Detroit a few years ago?"

"The same," she admitted. Water from the spill ran toward her stockinged toes. She braced the receiver between chin and shoulder trying to reach a cloth on the countertop.

"No kidding!"

"You said that, Jack," she reminded impatiently. She loved her brother dearly, but he'd always had a knack for calling at inopportune times.

"Yeah, wow!"

"Jack—" She'd have to nudge him along if she was ever going to get off the phone and tend to Herbie and the leafy collection languishing in the window. "Jack what's up—why did you call?"

"That's why I called," he replied cryptically. "I mean, Jackie's just started playing soccer. We've had a couple of practices already. I called to see if you can come to his scrimmage—you know, a practice game—Saturday morning."

"Gee, I don't know Jack. Things are at sixes and sevens for me with this assignment on my hands," she mused. "You know I'd love to see Jackie play—it doesn't seem possible he's old enough already!" At five years old, her adored, only nephew seemed hardly more than a toddler. "As far as I know the schedule's open, so I'll try and make it. Now I gotta go—"

"Wait!" he cried before she could get away. "Did you return that application to C.S.C. yet?" he demanded sternly.

"Now look, *little* brother," she replied menacingly, "don't get on me about that. I'm not sure about it. I need a little more time to think and pray, see what works out—"

"Well, don't wait too long," he cautioned.

"I promise, Jack. Now I really have to go," she sidled to the wall to replace the receiver. "You take care. Bye!" She hung up before he could protest.

"Whew!" She stooped and mopped up the spill, then headed for the plants again.

What a difference there was between their experience, she thought as she stood on the chair to water Herbie. At twenty-six she was the eldest, but Jack, a year younger, had been married for six years and a father for five. His job was finally working out for him too. Acceptance into the apprentice draftsman program at the Tech had settled down his restlessness after their father's death. She wished she were as sure of her future as he was. She dismissed a wayward pang of jealousy. She was truly happy for him.

The plants all watered, she returned with the pot to the kitchen windowsill and made herself a cup of tap water instant coffee. She was headed for the beckoning comfort of the overstuffed, blue-print chair when the phone rang again.

Neville? She didn't think so. Probably Jack again. What had he forgotten now? she wondered, shaking her head with a chuckle.

45

"Hello!" she said, surprised to hear how cheerful her voice sounded despite the hectic day. Her caller was surprised too.

"Yeah, Bree? It's me, Spence."

She froze halfway through the kitchen door. The irritation in his voice matched her own when she recognized it.

"Has the cave man made a move on you yet?"

"I'm not quite sure I know what you mean by that, Spence," she replied in kind. Part of her thrilled to the sound of his voice again. The other part resented his sneering intrusion.

"Get off it, Bree!" He pressed the subject, to her annoyance. "Professional jocks are always on the make. You know that 'cause you used to say the same thing."

"Well, I was wrong," she snapped. "I never knew any professionals before. Neville Ross has been a gentleman, and as I told you last night he's just business anyway."

"See that you remember that."

"Why did you call, Spence?" He was making her angry, and confusing her emotionally.

"I'd like to see you tonight." He lowered his voice seductively in the tone that used to weaken her resistance.

But it only annoyed her further.

"Whatever for?" she cried as a wicked prompting popped to mind. "Gena would like that!"

"I don't care what Gena likes!" he snapped back. "I'd just like to see you, that's all. We could go for a drive by the shore for old times' sake. There's no reason we can't still be friends."

The good old days weren't so good, she felt like reminding him, and it wasn't friendship he was after. He was slick all right. It was surprising how her insight into his character had grown.

Even so, a sudden longing seized her when she caught sight of his photo lying on her drawing board.

She never *had* gotten a frame for it.

"You mean you and Gena are quits already?" she needled, needing to strike back.

"No!—I—let's not talk about Gena. I miss you," he whispered huskily.

She wanted to believe him.

"Have you had the ring fixed yet?" She pushed the notion aside.

"I thought we could be adults about this, Bree." His voice took on a warning note. The phrase sounded like something from one of his psychology of management books. "Can I come up or not?"

Her bravado deserted her at the prospect. Spence at the end of a phone line was one thing, but in person? She turned her back to the drawing board and picture.

"No, Spence," she said in a rush. "I have too much to do. I'm tired, and tomorrow is another hectic day." She gave in to another mischievous prompting. "Besides, I have to wash my hair."

He didn't see the humor in the remark, and growling an impatient goodbye, he slammed down the phone. Bree put her hands to her burning face.

What's the matter with me? she thought. Breaking up with Spence yesterday hurt like crazy—it still does, but not as much. Am I so shallow I fall in and out of love *that* easily?

She reached behind her and found the photo with her hand. Slowly, methodically, she tore it in half again and again till the pieces spilled like confetti from her fingers.

She didn't need any reminders of her lapse in romantic judgment. His lack of faith was the reason for their break-up and had prevented her—perhaps even *preserved* her from totally committing her heart to him. No matter how tempted she might be, she knew she'd never go back to him.

This afternoon in the car with Neville had changed that.

With his name came his image, tousled hair and engaging smile and an unsettling thought. This part of his tour ended Sunday, and tomorrow was Wednesday. Their week together was half gone.

Chapter Five

Wednesday morning Brianne called ahead to make sure Neville was ready and waiting for her when she got there. This time, secure in the knowledge he was a man who wouldn't take advantage of the situation, she went directly to his room. Funny, she felt she knew him that well after so short an acquaintance.

"Brianne! Is that you?" Neville yelled through the door when she knocked. "No need to be so formal," he smiled, opening the door for her. "Next time just walk right in."

"That could prove embarrassing, don't you think?" she pointed out.

"For you or me?" he countered, wriggling his eyebrows.

Neville was strolling around with the phone—set in one hand, receiver in the other. He rolled his eyes toward the receiver and put it back to his ear.

"Yes, Gerry, I'm still here!" He laughed at something the caller said. "No, you needn't call back. It's nothing like that. Brianne is my escort—at least for now."

His eyes glinted with mischief while he watched Bree and smiled at Gerry's rejoinder, which she suspected was about her.

Piqued and a little uneasy, she raised her wrist and tapped her watch.

"Okay! Okay!" Chastened, he nodded. "Brianne is threatening to drag me out of here by the ear. Just have the papers ready when I see you. Sounds like you have it well in hand, so all I have to do is sign the—" With a quick look at Bree he changed the subject. "Then we're all set for tomorrow, right?"

The business settled, he hung up.

Brianne rose from her chair and picked up his khaki light-weight jacket from the sofa where he'd tossed it.

"We're running late again, Mr. Ross," Bree admonished playfully, "and while I suspect Mr. McBain overlooks your peccadilloes out of affection, the director of the film crew waiting for you will not."

"You're right," he grimaced, "so I'd better not forget this." He jammed his arms into the jacket with more utility than grace, shrugged it into place, and reached over to pick up a bound manuscript from the bureau. "Now, all I have to do is remember what's *in* it."

Bree took the car keys from her purse. As she brought them out, he took her hand, lifting the keys from her grasp.

"I'd like to drive if you've no objections," he said.

"Whatever," she shrugged, hoping he hadn't noticed the tiny jolt his touch caused. "I hope you know the area better than I do."

She tried to slip her hand from him, but he pulled it through the arm with the script tucked under it and held it there with his other hand as they went to the parking lot for the car.

He did know the area. His chatty reminiscences made the long drive out the Lodge Freeway to Milford seem shorter.

"I practically cut my teeth on the tires of prototype Mantas," he explained, talking about his father's part in developing one of the first American-production sports cars. At the Milford exit he turned right, passing through the tiny village of Milford and back into the surrounding rural countryside. At a place in the road where another road appeared to cross it, Neville turned right and drove about a quarter of a mile past a guard shack to a parking lot.

Though the turnoff had been unmarked, the lawn at the main entrance was trimmed and set with beds of red flowers, contrasting sharply with the uncultivated countryside around it.

Two large trucks and several cars were parked in one corner of the lot. A silver and burgundy Beauville van was parked near the entrance. McBain and a man in a brown uniform leaned against the van's open sliding door watching for them. McBain smiled broadly as Neville swung in beside him and turned off the engine.

"I wondered how long it would be before you took over," McBain said as he opened the door for Bree.

"Not that Brianne isn't an excellent chauffeur," Neville hastened to assure him, "but you know my impatience with being driven. Where in this gargantuan maze will we be filming?"

"You'll be doing your little bit at the high-speed loop, where we're headed right now. And speaking of impatient people," McBain said escorting Bree to the van, "you've got a pack of them waiting for you down at the site. The director and crew have been here since six a.m. setting up and getting some shots of the Manta in action. I tried to hold off the unveiling till you got here, but...."

Neville gave Bree a sheepish grin. "If that's calculated to make me feel guilty, it does!"

"Not at all," McBain said, "I know Miss Tyler has her hands full making sure you get to where you're supposed to be—on time." He paused. "This whole idea was helter-skelter to begin with. We didn't know till the last minute you'd be in town when we planned to

51

do the Manta spots, so I guess we should be glad we've got you at all."

Bypassing Neville, he held out a hand to assist Bree up the van's high step. She twitched up her navy front-buttoning straight skirt a bit and took hold of the seat rail with her other hand. Suddenly she was grasped around the waist by a pair of large hands and lifted easily into the van. She turned in time to see Neville throw McBain a wink as he climbed up after her.

Bree hurriedly seated herself on the far side of the center seat, Neville sliding after her to drape an arm casually across the seat's back. McBain took the seat beside the driver, and they were off.

There was a lot to see as they rolled through the rural setting. It looked as if someone had dropped the complicated track system down smack in the middle of someone's farm. Gently rolling, wooded green hills abounded. Though it was cooler out here than it had been in town, the day promised to heat up considerably. Mirages already shimmered off the road ahead of them in the warmth of the rising sun.

"Yes, she's something special." McBain was concluding a conversation Bree had missed while absorbed with the view from her window.

"Will Nev—Mr. Ross be able to drive the Manta himself?" she asked, curious.

"*No!*" both men answered in unified chagrin. McBain laughed ruefully.

"Anyone who drives on the road system out here has to have a special license," he explained. "I have one myself, but there's no way I could get one for Neville at this point, not till he's officially part of the—"

"This *is* quite a complex," Neville broke in but not before Bree caught the end of McBain's speech. He seemed to regard Neville's joining the company as more of a sure thing than her charge had indicated on the talk show yesterday.

"There's something going on here constantly," Neville went on. "I wish we had time for me to show you some of the labs. I'd like to see some of them myself. I suppose all the extra people at the track must be giving the security guys fits."

"That they are," McBain confirmed. "Company regulations won't allow anyone—even me—out here without an escort." He nodded his head at the driver.

"So we have an escort for the escort," Neville murmured.

"Not that it's likely to happen with Mr. McBain aboard," the driver spoke then, "but if you have any questions he can't answer feel free to ask."

"Providing they're not about top secret prototypes, right?" Neville added.

"Right!" the driver laughed. "But they've been moved far enough out of sight, so no one will be tempted to ask questions."

"I suppose the spies are at their worst this time of the year, just before the new models come out?" Neville mused.

Bree listened with interest. It was general knowledge in this automotive town that industrial spying went on. Newspapers and auto specialty magazines competed to see who'd be first to reveal the new designs. Now here she was, hearing it first hand.

"The spies are always bad," McBain laughed. "We keep building the walls higher, but they keep finding new vantage points."

They'd ridden for about ten minutes with Neville, McBain, and the driver swapping stories about the proving grounds when Bree began to get impatient.

"I never realized it was this big," she said to Neville who'd been leaning over her shoulder to look out her window.

They crossed a test area where several cars had light bars across their roofs with round red, yellow, and green lights on them.

"I believe it's an EPA test," Neville guessed, close to her ear. "The colors light up to indicate acceleration, deceleration, and braking activity."

"We've got about 128 miles of road system out here," McBain said.

"It seems as though we've come so far," Bree mused and then felt embarrassed when McBain laughed. She hadn't meant for him to hear that.

"Soon," he assured her. "It's too bad we don't have time to visit some of the labs," he said to Neville. "With your computer background you'd find the electromagnetic capability lab's work fascinating."

Bree hadn't known about Neville's interest in computers either. Apparently he'd had time to do more than just play soccer over the last few years. She didn't know him as well as she thought and reminded herself that she must take time to read his biography through.

"Here we are, Miss Tyler!" McBain shifted in his seat, unbuckling the belt as they crossed a bridge and rounded a hairpin turn to where a ramp branching left and right descended to a track.

While they were waiting for security to clear them and back one of the cars off the ramp for them to pass, a young man with a walkie-talkie ran up to one of the guards and both took off in a security car.

"It gets to be a hassle, filming in here," McBain said. "The crew can't bring the equipment truck on site, so if anything is forgotten, security has to run someone out to the parking lot to get it."

As they descended the ramp, Bree saw several vehicles and a large mobile home parked in a clear area near the banked track. A streak of silver flashed by on the track ahead of them, and she guessed she'd gotten her first glimpse of the twenty-fifth anniversary Manta.

A small army of people stood around talking and watching the crew mount a camera car with a boom on a set of tracks. That done, one of the crew took the car by the long handle extending from its back and pushed it back and forth to test it.

Their driver pulled up near the mobile home.

"I'll go check in with my people and let Martell know you're here," McBain said, hopping nimbly out of the van. He went over to a knot of people watching the Manta on the track, following what looked like a large pickup truck carrying a boom-mounted movie camera.

Neville rolled the van door open and descended, favoring his right knee. He turned and held his hands out for her.

"I think I can manage," she said, thinking he meant a repeat of his little feat in the parking lot.

But dismounting the precarious step gracefully—and modestly—in a straight skirt, buttoned slit notwithstanding, proved more difficult than she had thought. The skirt impeded her stride, and she tottered forward, grabbing frantically for the doorpost to steady herself.

"Careful!" Neville caught her to him and set her feet on the ground.

"Here now, that'll be enough of that." He smiled down at her. "We've got four more days to get through—I can't have you disabling yourself."

"That was stupid of me," she apologized, flushing with embarrassment and anger at herself. A quick glance assured her no one had noticed the incident.

"You mean—you didn't do it on purpose?" he feigned surprised.

She looked up to see the corners of his lips twitch.

"One of these days, Neville Ross," she threatened, wagging a finger at him. "I'm going to get you for your teasing."

"Promises, promises," he sighed disappointedly.

"You're incorrigible!"

"...and dashing, handsome, charming."

"Mr. Ross!" One of the crew members nearby detached himself from a group hovering around the mobile home. "You're wanted in makeup immediately!"

Neville sighed heavily. "Well, back to work." He leaned over to retrieve his script from the seat of the van. "You're in for a rare treat, a look at what goes into the making of a commercial, my dear."

"It looks absolutely fascinating!" Bree enthused, trying to see everything at once.

"Come along then." He took her hand, pulling her along into the trailer with him. "There's usually a ton of food in here, or you can get some coffee if you'd rather...."

A steady stream of people moved into and out of the trailer which Bree discovered was not only wardrobe, makeup, and cafeteria, but also the only on-site restroom as well. The makeup artist claimed Neville first, shooing him to her corner of the trailer. Bree grabbed an apple from the array of fresh fruit, vegetables, and candy bars and headed back outside to find a quieter vantage point.

She soon discovered there was a lot of sitting or standing around waiting involved in filming. Only a few people at a time were used for setting up the shots. Colored plastic milk crates made impromptu seats for anyone who chose to sit while the director finished his work on the track.

McBain stood with a group of well-dressed people near a TV monitor a little way behind the camera car on tracks. Some of them also sat on the countless milk crates.

Finally the Manta and then the camera pulled off the track. Two men and a woman jumped down from the back of the truck to be joined by the Manta's driver, a tall, lean young man in blue slacks and white shirt with sleeves rolled up to the elbows. Squinting against the sun's glare reflecting off the silver surface, he walked slowly around his car, giving it a critical once-over.

"There! That didn't take so long." Neville popped jovially out the trailer door. He raised a hand to his face to scratch his chin, caught himself, and lowered it again with a frown. "I'd forgotten how much I hate this makeup."

Wardrobe had fitted him out in a double-breasted navy blazer with brass buttons, navy tie, and white shirt topping off gray slacks. He looked the picture of the upwardly mobile young professional, which in fact he was.

McBain detached himself from the group at the monitor to jog over to the director. Both started over to where Neville stood with Bree.

"Neville, you remember Kurt from our Monday night meeting," McBain introduced the director simply while the two shook hands.

Apart from a mop of wildly curling hair surmounted by a pair of silver-lensed, aviator-style sunglasses, Martell appeared unexpectedly ordinary. He wore an unremarkable khaki, multi-pocketed shirt and tan jeans.

He could at least have worn riding boots or a beret, Bree grinned to herself.

"And this is Bruce Watt, the developmental engineer in charge of our latest offspring." McBain stepped aside for the Manta's driver to join the circle.

"I've been looking forward to meeting you, Ross." Watt said, pumping Neville's hand with enthusiasm while a big grin split his freckled face. "I've been an admirer of your father's work on the Manta."

"Well!" Neville said, gratified. "I think we'll get along famously, Watt. Gentlemen," he reached behind him to encircle Bree with his arm and drew her forward to their notice, "My nanny for the week, Brianne Tyler."

That he said it with a perfectly straight face drew chuckles from the other men, but Bree wanted to strangle him.

"Time's wasting," Martell reminded them, "and I only have a limited amount of yours, Ross, so let's get back to business. We have to finish as much as possible today since 'her highness' won't hit town till Friday—"

More snickers as they moved off, heads together over the script, but Bree noticed a tightening of the lines around Neville's mouth at the reference to 'her highness.' Who was she?

"Would you like to see the Manta?"

Bree turned to find Watt hovering uncertainly behind her. They'd been left to mill around with the rest of the crew.

"I'd love to!" Bree said with a bright smile. "That was *you* driving for the filming just now, wasn't it?"

"Yeah." He laughed shyly and joked, "I'm a star!"

"It must be very exciting."

"No, the exciting part was seeing it come to life, from the first sketches to the final testing," he confided, leading the way to the car at trackside.

"Yes," Bree agreed wistfully, thinking of her own creative endeavors. "Nothing can beat seeing an idea take form and become a reality in its own right...but tell me what you've got here."

Their presence at the car was an invitation to other crew members to wander in for a closer look at the Manta's new design.

Bruce walked around it first, explaining changes to revolutionize it for its twenty-fifth birthday. It still had the aerodynamically efficient clamshell hood, but they'd changed the flip-up headlights to cut down wind resistance. By now Bruce had a willing audience and held court accordingly so that Bree's head began to swim with technical jargon.

"...multicolored, electronic, liquid crystal readouts...fiberglass monoleaf transverse..."

She backed off to stroll around the car for an overall impression. And it was impressive!

Long, low, and sleek, the tapered rear end and clamshell hood combined to give the impression of the ray that inspired it. The cockpit appeared to be all glass.

58

Only a narrow strip of silver over the seats broke the flowing curve of windshield and rear hatch. In front, in the center of the designed-in bumper, a long flat louvered oval angled downward, finalizing the Manta image.

Brilliant sunlight sparkled over glass, trim, paint. Leaning closer Bree saw metallic silver flecks accounting for the gleaming, gemlike finish.

Bruce had gotten in the car to demonstrate how to pop the rear hatch when Neville reappeared at Bree's side.

"Dad would be proud," he murmured over her shoulder. He drew her over to the open door for a look into the cockpit.

"Chrome!" Bruce scoffed at Neville's comment on the silver-rimmed dials and gauges set into the black panel. "Chrome nothing! This job's special all the way. That's sterling silver, in honor of this august occasion."

Neville rolled his eyes, properly impressed.

"They should furnish a lifetime supply of Tarnex with it," he whispered irreverently to Bree.

"All right, everybody." Martell strode up. "Do you think we might possibly clear the area so we could get some work done today?" The terse question was the signal for everyone to scurry away while he returned to the camera car.

It was almost three by the time they reached the headquarters building in the New Center area. Bree was glad Neville drove again. The maze of one-way streets near the heavily trafficked Grand Boulevard-Woodward intersection reminded Bree of a rabbit warren, and there was a lot of activity for midafternoon. Office workers bustled from one tall building to another alongside impressive executives carrying expensive briefcases. Neville pulled into a metered parking place across from the east entrance of the building and hustled them across the street.

Once inside, Bree gasped, craning her neck to see the ornate embossed work on the corridor's ceiling.

"I'd forgotten how beautiful it is down here," she explained sheepishly to Neville's inquiring look.

"It is indeed," he agreed, glancing up at the blue and gold paneled ceiling with its floral motifs.

They took an elevator to the fourteenth floor, then hesitated while Neville got his bearings in the hall lobby.

"Well!" A tall, distinguished-looking dark man in a summer-weight blue suit came up behind them. "A celebrity who's punctual!"

"You've no idea how I detest being called a celebrity," Neville winced. "Mike, this is Brianne Tyler, my friend and escort for this business."

"Oh!" Bree was caught off guard when Mike held out a hand to her. She'd braced herself to be called a nanny again. "Sorry, I was daydreaming, I guess," she apologized.

"Brianne," Mike acknowledged warmly with a smile that deepened the laugh lines around the mouth and eyes.

"Mike Kozara, another old friend. I'm afraid you're going to be meeting a lot of them before this ordeal is over," Neville laughed. "There's no point in your hanging around here waiting for me, so why don't you head home and get ready for our dinner engagement. Then you can pick me up at the hotel."

"What time?" Bree prompted as two men joined Mike and distracted Neville.

He smiled mysteriously at her.

"For what I have planned, you'd better make it 5:45."

She gave him a dubious look, checking her watch.

"This won't take long, and I'll catch a ride with someone—"

"You're the boss," she said, shaking her head.

"*Ms.* Tyler!" he said immediately. "I never thought

60

I'd ever hear you say that!"

"*Figuratively* speaking," she threw back over her shoulder at him as she headed for the elevators.

"Roger!" she heard Neville exclaim behind her. "Good to see you again!"

"Ross," the man returned, "we've just been going over the details." Then he added a puzzler, a strange thing to say to someone only in town plugging an automobile for a commercial. "I hear you've decided to locate in Birmingham. If you're half as good as your father at his speciality, you'll be more than welcome with us."

Chapter Six

"I feel like I've spent half my life ferrying between the apartment and this hotel," Bree muttered to herself, trudging back through the lobby to the elevator that evening.

She shook out a silk knit antique shawl that matched the color of her cream chiffon dinner dress and threw it around her shoulders to free her hands. The corner of a small cellophane bag containing her surprise for Neville caught in the shawl's delicate threads. She extricated it and pressed the elevator button, smiling to herself as she rehearsed the line with which she intended to present her gift to him.

He opened the door just as she arrived and raised a hand to knock. His eyes widened in appreciation as they fell on her, but before he could comment she whipped the cellophane wrapper up between them.

"What's *this?*" he asked suspiciously taking it between thumb and forefinger by its stapled end.

"I always bring my dates flowers." Bree giggled, sweeping past him into the room.

He looked up from under his lashes, a slow smile curving his lips as he took the single red rosebud out of its wrapping.

"Very appropriate," he murmured, turning it between his fingers in the light. "But now, how do I look?" He held his arms wide and pivoted slowly. "A bit more appropriate, I hope, in keeping with your image of what a proper businessman should look like?"

Her eyes examined him, taking in the dark blue pinstripe suit cut narrow at the waist and smooth over the slim hips, making him seem even taller than he already was. A crisp white shirt and red club tie completed his outfit.

"Monumental!" she breathed in approving awe.

For the third time that day, Neville took over the driving chore when they returned to the car, seating Brianne in the passenger side with authority.

"I thought you might like a break in the routine," he said, sliding the driver's seat back to accommodate his height.

"How did you manage to—" Brianne stopped to readjust her seat to keep from having to lean forward to see him when he talked. He grinned in amusement.

"I had a little time after the meeting to do some shopping," he answered her unfinished question.

She was amazed at how easily he found his way around the Detroit freeways and said so.

"You forget," he said, "I had to live here when I played for Detroit."

When he headed for Southfield Road, she guessed their destination was one of the many posh restaurants downtown. Confirming her suspicion, he swung left when the road divided and headed south on Lodge Freeway.

"I've always liked that dome," he said, nodding to the serrated, gleaming gold roof of St. John's Armenian Church above the treetops nestled in the fork of the divide. "Did you know the roof is made of real gold?"

"No!" Brianne was surprised. "I wondered about that because it shines differently—like real gold. But then, I don't know too much about this part of town. I'm totally at sea around here."

"Funny you should choose that analogy," he chuckled. "What part of town do you call home?" He reached over to punch on the air conditioner full blast.

"I grew up on the east side, by the old City Airport." She drew the shawl tighter around her shoulders against the assault of cold air from the vents. "You know, the little one?"

With a glance at her he leaned over again to adjust the blower speed and tap the vents away from her. The scent of his cologne wafted up to her on the breeze.

Patchouli, she analyzed. *I wonder if that sharp, clean smell is patchouli?*

"Then we moved back to the place where I grew up, at least till I was twelve, when Dad transferred back to Melbourne."

"Hm?" Embarrassed, Bree realized she'd missed half of what he'd said while she was busily analyzing his scent.

He laughed. "So much for my interesting conversation!"

"No, really, I was distracted by a thought for a minute," she apologized. "I'm sorry."

"Then you'll have to do penance by hanging on my every word for the rest of the evening, and I'll quiz you later to see if you listened."

"That's only fair," she returned.

They'd exited the Lodge and were snaking through downtown streets Bree barely remembered from Sunday drives with her family. Their destination now appeared to be the riverfront.

Bree tried to remember what restaurants were on the river but soon gave up. Eating out at nice places had not been a part of her recent experience. She'd been lucky not to wind up at White Castle when Spence took her out for dinner.

Nuts! she thought. *Go away, Spencer Kenyon.*

"I was telling you about my thrilling childhood in Oakland County," Neville picked up the thread of his thoughts, "but the rerun will have to wait till we're

65

aboard. Right now I have to concentrate on this road to make sure it goes where I think it does! I don't remember these one-way streets."

He navigated a turn onto Jefferson Avenue and passed the black marble facade of Ford Auditorium. Coming to the stoplight at the Renaissance Center, he made two quick rights and a left, pulling into the parking garage across from the Westin Hotel's lobby.

Bree assumed then that they were going to one of the restaurants in the hotel, hopefully the revolving one at the hotel's summit. The view of the river and rolling vistas of Windsor across it would be spectacular at twilight.

But after they'd parked, Neville steered her toward a door on the opposite side of the garage. They emerged and walked a little way till Bree saw a ship moored at the dock before them. At first glance it looked like a miniature cruise ship, its blue and white hull rising with the swell of the river. Large square windows rather than the standard round portholes ran the length of the hull's broad blue band at dock level. The upper enclosed deck, shorter to allow an open observation area along its surrounding rail, was also blue, as were the third level deck and the pilot's cabin. Colorful pennants strung from bow to stern fluttered on the breeze blowing from up river, giving the whole a festive appearance.

On the point of the prow was painted the gold star that named the line and the ship, the *Star of Detroit.*

"Oh!" Bree sighed in wonder.

"Surprised?" Neville asked, watching her reaction. "A pleasant surprise I hope. You haven't been on the *Star* yet have you? That Kenyon hasn't—"

Bree thrilled to the note of jealousy in his voice—it *was* jealousy, wasn't it? "No!" she hastened to assure him. "It's just—this is one of those places I've heard so much about and wanted to see but never had the opportunity. And it's a little out of Spence's league.

Spence would never dream of bringing me here unless I badgered him, in which case he'd remind me every few minutes what a hardship it was."

Bree was immediately sorry she'd spoken so bitterly. Neville, of course, picked up on it.

"The bloom of your infatuation with young Lochinvar has worn off, I see," he observed with acute interest, but she thought she saw sympathy in his glance as they started across the walkway to board.

She looked warily at the murky green of the water undulating below them.

He tucked her hand reassuringly into the bend of his arm. "I'm an excellent swimmer," he said dryly.

The hostess, in a tailored white nautical jacket with gold braid epaulettes, took their tickets and escorted them aboard.

They passed through the observation cooking area amidship on the main deck, with its stoves in full view of diners who watched while chefs in white bustled to prepare salads and desserts. At the front of the area, three huge, round copper domes with brass pineapple finials sat on white tiled countertops trimmed with natural wood.

"It looks so warm and inviting," Bree commented. "I love all the copper and wood!"

The tables were covered with white linen cloths; the chairs were unusually fine for a restaurant. Of contemporary Danish design, they had vertically slatted backs from top rail to blue carpeted floor. The color scheme throughout was the blue and white of the ship itself.

Neville and Bree mounted a staircase to the upper-level dining room. The table the hostess led them to was near the dance floor and bandstand at the front of the ship, on the *port* side, Neville pointed out with a knowing wink.

"There's something romantic about dining on a ship," Bree enthused as he seated her. Shoulder height

Araca palms on both sides set their table apart from those closest to it.

"I was hoping you'd think so," he replied.

"But it's not very businesslike."

"Business be hanged! Tonight is for pleasure. This table will be fine, thank you."

The hostess smiled. "Your captain will be with you shortly. You're welcome to move about the vessel before or after your meal, but we do ask that you remain seated once you've ordered."

"So our dinner doesn't get cold while we're out galavanting," Neville leaned over to whisper.

"Right!" the hostess laughed. Then she hurried back to her post.

"Good evening, sir, ma'am. My name is Carl, and I'm your captain this evening." A young man in similar uniform greeted them. "Would you care for a cocktail before dinner?"

"If you're the captain, who's driving this boat?" Neville asked mischievously.

A broad grin split Carl's face, highlighting deep dimples in his cheeks.

"*He* is!" He jerked a thumb toward a nearby speaker as the captain's voice came on to welcome them aboard and give the safety regulations for the cruise.

"Did you care for anything to drink?" Neville asked Bree, returning to Carl's question.

"No, thank you."

"I don't care for anything, either," he said. "Perhaps we should go ahead and order—unless you'd like to see the ship first?" He looked up at her expectantly, but for once they were in agreement about food.

"No!" she said honestly. "I'm famished!"

"A woman after my own heart," he teased again.

"We specialize in American cuisine," Carl said, going over the menu for them, but Neville decided quickly on shrimp remoulade with creole sauce to start with, pasta salad, and an entrée of beef tenderloin on a bed of Virginia him.

"It all sounds so good!" Bree agonized over her decision. At a lifting of his eyebrows and a slow teasing grin from Neville, she chose the same appetizer and salad but chicken and pecan fettucine for her main course.

"Well, this is special," she explained with a shrug, toying with the fresh flower centerpiece in its squat blue vase. "It isn't *every* day I'm taken to dinner by a celebrity who's handsome, charming, dashing—"

He laughed and leaned back to look at her pensively.

"Your own words," she reminded him.

"It isn't the first time they've been used against me!"

The darkness of his suit, contrasted with his tanned blond coloring, seemed to intensify the blue of his eyes. Bree found the effect devastating. She looked away. *He's just business, Tyler.* She reminded herself ruthlessly. *Just business—and don't forget it.*

To cover her momentary confusion and regain her composure she took the fan-folded blue napkin off the blue-rimmed white plate and smoothed it over her lap. When she looked up he'd taken a spray of baby's breath from the carnation arrangement and, leaning across the table, he tucked it into her hair. She had worn it swept up tonight except for a few stubborn tendrils that curled along her neck which gleamed against the clinging chiffon of her dress at its delicate V closure.

"Though I like your hair down, it's quite lovely like this, showing off your classic features," he mused approvingly.

Bree steeled herself to meet the blue gaze without flinching or blushing.

"Do you make it a point to tell all your escorts that?" she countered coyly. She thought she had him figured now. His boldness, the startling frankness was calculated to get a reaction from women. Witness the book-signing session at Dayton's. It was a game for him, an accomplished flirt, to unsettle them, make them blush and giggle at his attentions.

"No, I don't think that would have gone over too well with Hugo." His mouth curved into a most devastating smile while he held her eyes captive in his cerulean gaze. "He was bald."

Bree laughed in spite of herself. Calculated flirt or not, he was fun to be with—all the more reason to be on guard against his gentle lures. It would be unthinkable if, in *her* little game of using him to get over Spence, she ended up falling in love with Neville instead. Recognizing the possibility of such a thing made her uneasy, but she hastily dismissed the thought and looked him in the eyes, tossing her head with a laugh.

He'd expected a different reaction.

"I can assure you my dear, his lack of hair was no laughing matter to him!" he tried again but the "charmer" smile slipped to the old irreverent grin she preferred.

She turned her attention to the little pot of herbs on the broad, woodlike windowsill.

"Chives." She identified them while he regarded her with a puzzled look. "They used to grow wild in the grass where I went to college. Every time the grass was cut it smelled like a salad."

"Indeed!" Neville said with interest. "A timely observation since I was about to demand an autobiographical account from you. Turnabout's fair play, and I know you've got me down to the dot on the 'i' in 'Neville' in that biography you insist on carrying around."

He flicked a hand toward her gold mesh bag and the edges of typed pages peeping from one corner of the clasp.

She did blush then, not because she knew all about him, but because she didn't. He smiled in triumph.

70

"May I see it?" He held out a hand to her. She handed it to him, watching his face register amusement, incredulity, and finally chagrin at what he read.

"Is there something in it you didn't want printed?"

"No," he said, chuckling. "I'm not concerned so much by what's said as what could have been—and wasn't!"

He took her purse out of her hands, stuffed the bio back into it, and snapped it shut.

"Now, enough of 'Digger' Ross—I want to hear about Brianne Tyler."

"Really," she demurred uneasily, "there's nothing to tell. My life has been quite boringly ordinary."

"Nonsense." He cut her off. "No one is boringly ordinary. And you, my dear, I've felt from the first, are most extraordinary."

He'd lifted her hand from the table to his lips briefly and back again as he spoke, keeping it in his hand. A surge of confusing emotions threatened to overturn her composure, but Brianne returned his languid gaze with a secret taunting smile. She knew what his game was, however much an annoying little part of her heart began to wish he meant it.

"You asked for it. Where shall I begin?"

"The beginning is always nice." Leaning forward he propped his arms on the table, rested his chin on one hand, and fixed her with a rapt look.

She shrugged, acutely conscious of her hand still in his on the table.

"All right. First, I'm the eldest of five children, four boys and one girl—me."

"My dear," he called her that a lot, "you're stating the obvious."

"—and let me warn you *Mr.* Ross, I'm accustomed to running my brothers like a race."

"There, you see? You've justified my first impressions already. Not having had any siblings myself, I shall find your experiences quite enlightening."

He was enjoying this, Bree noticed. But then, so was she. She laughed, relaxing more. It would make her game that much more exciting and challenging, to outwit the rogue and charm the charmer.

Dinner arrived, and while Carl and his junior waiter served and retreated, she recounted her childhood in an old east side ethnic neighborhood. He laughed with delight, plying her with bits of spicy shrimp from his appetizer in exchange for her seafood ravioli. He seemed genuinely interested as she told of her family squabbles and exploits that had landed them all in trouble at various times with parents and neighbors.

"We had our own little gang, in a sense," she mused affectionately as Carl replaced appetizers with salads. "Despite all the fights, we knew we could count on one another when the going got tough...."

Neville watched, a wistful expression in his eyes. An unnamed longing glimmered in his eyes as she spoke of her family life, but all he said was, "You were very fortunate."

Abruptly breaking the mood, he sat up and stretched.

"Will I get to meet this poor gaggle of males you've dominated all these years?"

She couldn't tell from the laughing light in his eyes if he was serious or not. Light flirtation didn't usually entail taking the "flirtee" home to meet mother.

"It would serve you right if I did," she threatened. "They'd tease you unmercifully about your accent—"

"*My* accent?"

"—and call you a kangaroo jockey—"

"I've never ridden a kangaroo in my life! And no self-respecting kangaroo would tolerate such foolishness," he objected indignantly. "Don't think that will scare me off, though!"

"If you're that intent on meeting them, I'll take you home. You'll easily intimidate the guys with your height, and if that doesn't do it, I suppose you could just *sit* on them—"

"There you go!" Neville approved. "You make it sound like such fun I can hardly wait. When do we go?"

"Now wait!" she said as Carl appeared again, with their steaming entrées. "You're booked so heavily it'll take some maneuvering to squeeze in any kind of an extra stop—"

"But I have every confidence in your ability to do so." He knew he'd put her on the spot and was enjoying it as he cut into his tenderloin of beef with relish.

Neville one, Bree zip, she thought.

"You mentioned you went to college, where?"

"A small Bible college in the south," she said, launching into a description of her academic experience. It seemed to surprise him. "It was the high point of my life I guess."

"But of course you hadn't met *me* yet!"

She laughed. "I didn't go to college right after high school. My dad died shortly after I graduated, and it threw us a little."

"A little?" he said, with a look of disbelief and concern. "I should think it was a devastating experience."

"It could have been," she murmured thoughtfully. Should she mention her faith, speak of how God had brought them through it relatively intact? The evening was going smoothly, she felt reluctant to bring it up. But she knew she couldn't take credit for the new admiration she saw dawning in his eyes. She couldn't deny her Lord or faith in Him that pulled them through.

"It could have been, but it wasn't. Why?" The flirtatious facade was dropped. A look of intent inquiry took its place. He was just Neville now, the self she knew he showed to few people.

She told him simply and quietly how God had been like a hedge around the family, taking care of their every need in the confusing times. Care and provision by Christian friends had tided them over till the financial tangles were finally resolved. She looked up to see what effect these disclosures had on him and saw "the look," the skepticism she'd experienced from Spence. But it passed.

He nodded and said encouragingly, "Go on."

"Really, that's all there is," she said, taking up her fork again.

"You remind me of someone."

"Who?" She saw a new warmth in his eyes before his quicksilver change of expression.

"My mother."

Carl's return to inquire about dessert interrupted the conversation again, and when he left with their order, Neville changed the subject.

"Here we are letting a perfectly marvelous cruise slip away from us! Why don't we go inspect the rest of the ship now? It would be a shame to waste a beautiful evening indoors."

"You're right. Besides," Bree confessed, "I haven't read that biography yet; I'd much rather hear it from you."

She gave him her most appealing look and laughed at his exasperated grimace. But as they ambled arm in arm out of the dining room and onto the deck, he gave an accounting of his childhood.

His disappointment at the family's return to Australia was almost tangible. His father's decision that it was time for him to follow Ross family tradition and attend school and university in England only increased his restlessness. He'd taken a degree at Cambridge—he didn't say in what—but the lure of professional soccer proved too strong to resist. For all its excitement and adulation even that wore thin after a while.

"One of the drawbacks of that sort of existence was whenever I met someone whose friendship I wanted to cultivate, it was time to move on again."

"Meaning female someones?" Bree instantly regretted the innocent question.

"Is that jealousy I hear?" He caught her elbow, swinging her around to face him. They'd moved from the upper deck to the observation deck, and in the clear sky over his shoulder stars gleamed like little points of light against the midnight blue.

"No! I mean—" she fumbled, punctuating her efforts with helpless gestures. "I mean, it's only natural—"

"I know what you meant," he apologized, taking her hands to still them, "but *do* be jealous—I love it. It's terribly flattering."

She wrinkled her nose at him.

"Establishing friendships of any kind has been almost impossible for the past ten years, but hopefully that part of my life is over," he sighed distractedly, staring over the water at distant lights on shore.

The *Star* had reached its turning point in Lake St. Clair and headed around for the return to Detroit. "I'm looking forward to settling into some sort of normalcy now. With the money from this book and commercial, I can finally pursue the things that really matter."

Bree started to ask what he planned to accomplish but he spun her around gently, putting his arms around her and drawing her to him. As he nuzzled the hair around her face, the faint smell of his Polo cologne mingling with the wet breeze from the river tantalized her nostrils. She heard the warning in her mind against his closeness but felt powerless to resist.

"It's beautiful over there," his mellifluous voice murmured close to her ear, and she knew she was reaching the point of no return.

"Too chilly for you?" he asked when she shivered.

"No," her mind searched frantically for a safe, coherent thought. "I was just remembering I've always liked the view across the river of the Canadian side. It

75

seems so tranquil compared to busy Detroit. When we were kids my folks used to take us for drives along the lake shore. Especially in the summer, at night, to get away from the heat in the city. The water seemed to come right up to the road, and I was always afraid we'd drive right off into it!" She shivered again at the memory, and he hugged her tight, rocking her slightly.

She hoped the babbling didn't reveal her true state of mind. One of the first things she'd learned about him was his uncanny knack for seeing more than he let on. If he'd been trying to unsettle her, he couldn't have picked a better way. His personal magnetism, almost more than his physical presence, was overpowering.

Lulled by the sound of the water lapping against the ship, she closed her eyes and leaned her head back against his wide shoulder.

Was this all part of the game for him, too? The shore lights wavered through sudden tears. Well, it wasn't part of her game. *You're not going to reduce me to the level of a squealing, fainting groupie, Neville Ross,* she thought. She pulled away from him.

"What is it?" His voice expressed concern. He leaned over the rail trying to see her face. "Did I do something wrong? If I did, it certainly wasn't my intention. Look at me, Brianne...."

She turned with reluctance.

"I look forward to the time we spend together. I wouldn't for the world do anything to jeopardize that or your good opinion of me. Am I forgiven?"

He was so sincere, and the anxious eyes watching her were so blue. She swallowed hard. "Of course. I guess I should remember you find me more attractive than the Chicago wrestler..."

He laughed and hugged her quickly as the ship passed under the Ambassador Bridge and turned toward Hart Plaza.

They returned to the dining room, but Bree resolved to put a closer guard on her rebellious heart. She was finding Neville much more attractive and tempting than she'd anticipated.

Their old camaraderie restored, he helped her don the shawl again. She was distracted from his comments about the docking procedure by the sound of a laugh, throaty and seductive, across the room. Standing now she could see the couple who had been hidden behind the large brass espresso machine on the serving island amidship earlier. The young woman, not more than twenty-one, if that, leaned across the table twirling her long-stemmed glass languidly as she hung on every word from her entranced companion. One exquisitely manicured hand reached up to smooth a long strand of shimmering red-gold hair back to its sleek cascade below her shoulders. Whisper-thin and couture-clad, she brought to mind a recent commercial and a conversation she'd had at the Tech.

"Doesn't that woman look just like Jennifer Thrale, the model?" she whispered, calling Neville's attention to the scene across the room. "And did you hear she's supposed to be coming from London to finish the commercial with you later this week?"

She immediately wished she could take it back. He turned his head sharply at mention of the popular model's name, his easygoing demeanor changed. She could almost see the door of his mind slam shut behind his eyes. He looked away and stood motionless for a brief instant. She couldn't have put a more effective damper on his attentions if she'd tried.

"Come along," he said in a monotone. He picked up his change from the tray on the table, carelessly stuffing it in his pocket. When they passed by the table of the model's look-alike, he looked straight ahead to avoid seeing her interested glance.

Through the gauntlet of the young crew members who lined up on either side of the gangway to say good night, he shepherded her in silence. Once in the car, he jammed the key into the ignition with such force she feared he'd broken it. But with a vicious twist of the starter he revved the engine, paid the parking attendant, and took off out of the garage with tires squealing.

This mercurial change in mood frightened her, partly because she felt she'd inadvertently caused it. It was such a radical departure from the norm for him! She felt miserable. Not knowing what to say, she decided it was probably best to say nothing.

In the glare of streetlights she caught glimpses of his face, withdrawn and tight. He was locked in some private world, a stranger to her now. She was uncomfortable, feeling like an intruder. With a start of alarm, she recognized the route he'd taken.

Why on earth did you take the long way out of Woodward if you'd rather be alone? she questioned silently. Escort duty or not, tender leanings of her heart notwithstanding, she only wanted to get home now. Perhaps tomorrow he would be his old cheerful, teasing self again, and they could get through the rest of the week tolerably.

She sighed, and he shot her a quick glance.

Funny. A few hours earlier she'd not wanted to think about his leaving at the end of the week.

He looked at her once or twice more without speaking as he drove. She wanted to reach over and touch his hand, to make some show of understanding, but didn't for fear of a rebuff.

Coward! her mind accused, especially after he'd been so close, so warm just a few minutes before. Sinking into her own thoughts, she wondered, *Do we ever really know another person, or do we deceive ourselves into thinking we do?*

After what seemed an eternity of silence, Neville turned off Woodward onto another busy street and made a few more turns. In the darkness she could make out an old established neighborhood of Woodward. The tall trees and stately houses were set well back from the road. For a moment, she was afraid he was headed for McBain's. How would she explain his pet celebrity's black mood should they confront him at this hour?

She looked quickly at Neville, but all his concentration was on the winding road ahead of them. She caught the glimmer of moonlight on water when they rounded another curve. He pulled up along a steep bank of a small lake and turned off the engine. Beautiful sprawling homes, ranches and colonials, looked out onto the lake from across the road behind them.

Neville got out without a word and came around for her.

"I hope you don't mind," he said shortly. The distracted frown still pulled his mouth down, but the words were an effort to re-establish communications.

He held her hand on his arm as was his usual custom, for comfort as well as guidance in the dark, she realized. He led her around on the narrow strip of grass that served as a lakeside park. She felt her affection for him rise to supplant her misgivings. Even in this melancholy withdrawn state, he wanted her to know he was aware of her presence, perhaps even desired it.

The grass widened farther on, and beyond a copse of deeply shadowed trees a small pier jutted out into the water. He watched the faint wind ripple the surface of the water while they walked out onto the pier. Turning abruptly, he leaned back against the pier's metal rail and stared hard in the direction of the homes across the street, trying to penetrate the darkness. Following the direction of his gaze, Bree could see nothing to warrant such scrutiny.

He turned to her. The clouded, closed expression was gone, but he still looked sad when he smiled wistfully at her.

She was glad he couldn't hear the commotion in her chest when he suddenly took her face in his hands.

"This is a very special place for me," he said, his voice barely audible over the rustling of wind and leaves in the nearby trees. "The Jennifer Thrales of this world would never appreciate it as I do—but I thought Brianne Tyler might."

This time he did kiss her, briefly but lingeringly on the lips.

Chapter Seven

Snap out of it, Tyler! Brianne frowned at her image as she brushed her hair before the bathroom mirror the next morning. The events of the previous evening—especially at the lake—still seemed more dreamlike than real. The kiss had shaken her, even though she realized now she'd wanted him to kiss her.

Neville had paused when he'd lifted his head from the kiss. In the light reflected from the lake, Bree had seen the pensive expression again looking into his eyes and she'd wished she could read him as easily as he read her. He had made a move as if to kiss her again when she finally got her treacherous heart back in hand.

"Now I know you didn't do that to the Chicago boxer!" she had laughed shakily, taking his wrists in her hands. Not only had the move prevented the second kiss, which she knew she couldn't handle, but it had also broken the mood nicely. "You have an early brunch date with some sports writers at the press club, Mr. Ross—we'd better get you home. It's already very late."

His fingers, those long fingers that could palm a soccer ball with ease, then curled in her hair, caressing the nape of her neck.

"No, I'm sure Hugo wouldn't have appreciated be-

81

ing kissed. And you're right. It *is* late."

He'd gripped her elbow lightly, and they'd chatted intermittently on the way back to the car. Then, as he helped her back in he'd given her another thoughtful, sweeping look and said inexplicably, "Matter of fact it's probably *too* late, for me."

It was that as well as the subtle change in him this morning when she'd picked him up and delivered him to the sports writers' meeting that made her dwell on the incident. He had seemed more attentive and less a tease than before.

"Tyler." She put the brush down to lean both hands on the vanity "It's a game—just a game. He's just amusing himself with this flirtation the same as you are."

But the nagging doubt in the back of her mind refused to go away.

"Well, I don't have time to stand here and argue with you!" She sniffed at her reflection, and turning her back on it, she huffed out of the bathroom and down the hall to the kitchen.

"Guess I could straighten up a bit," she said, surveying the wreckage of three hectic days. Empty coffee cups and toast crumbs lined the butcher block counter. Karen, a compulsive neatnik, would absolutely freak if she saw the mess.

Brianne grabbed a sponge and swept the counter top, rinsing out the cups and stowing them in the dishwasher. She started it and then puttered to the living room. Finding that the activity diverted her mind from troublesome questions, she doubled her efforts and attacked the clutter around her drawing board and easel in an all-out cleaning blitz.

Finally there was nothing left to do. She packed the vacuum away in the closest and stood back to survey the cozy, neat living room. She'd tend to the laundry later.

Thank goodness Karen had invited her to move in. It would have been difficult to move back home, ousting

82

two brothers from her old room to do so. She preferred the peace and quiet here to the boisterous confusion there. Besides, she would have felt like a kid again living under her mother's roof, not like an adult living and making it on her own.

The room looked warm and inviting with its dark, wood-trimmed colonial-style furniture. The upholstery pattern was small and neat, like Karen: beige and rust on blue, matching the drapes at the bay window and the overstuffed chair with its short, squat ottoman. Brass lamps gleamed on tables at each end of the sofa in the filtered light of midafternoon. Herbie looked perkier, too, for having been shielded from the sun the past couple of days when she'd remembered to pull down the fabric shade that contrasted the upholstery.

The room looked so inviting Bree ambled over the plush, russet carpet to the chair and dropped into it, maneuvering the ottoman with her feet to just the right position for her legs. It felt good just to sit and do nothing, not even think, after the furious pace she'd been going. Her body tingled with the slowdown after the rush of cleaning, and she ran one hand over the smooth surface of the drop-leaf table beside her. The smell of the lemon-scented polish reminded her stomach she hadn't eaten yet.

"Later," she told it. "You could use a little starvation after last night!"

She grinned to herself, drumming her fingertips on the table top. They came to an abrupt halt when she spied her devotional book. She had planned to curl up here and do her reading this morning, but in the usual rush of getting up late she had foregone it. Now was a good time to read the Scripture selections for the day.

Brianne picked up her book, running a finger over the worn spine held intact by several layers of strapping tape. Too bad it was out of print. It would just have to be rebound someday.

She turned to the page for Thursday and read the theme verse: "Whoso trusteth in the Lord, happy is he." Her eyes ran down the page quickly reading the rest of the Scriptures with the theme of trust.

Remembering her thoughts about Neville, she wondered if she was trying to figure things out without putting her trust in the Lord's judgment. Was she trusting herself to get out of a situation she knew she couldn't handle?

The doorbell rang. Irritated at the interruption, she padded to the door and pulled it open as far as the chair allowed.

"Yes? What is—Spence!" Her heart jumped.

He looked as heartbreakingly handsome as ever, the crisp blue of his eyes nearly matching the color of his shirt. His unbuttoned collar revealed a tuft of dark hair. His tweed sport jacket indicated to her that it was one of his light days, one in which he didn't have to impress any really important clients by wearing a suit. But what was he doing on her doorstep in the middle of the day?

"Hi, Bree. May I come in?"

No! Bree thought. *You don't have any right to be here, much less come in!* But she said, "Sure...I guess. I have a while yet before I have to pick up Neville...."

At her mention of Neville Ross, Spence's grin froze. He brushed past Brianne to fling across the foyer, the heels of his shoes clicking sharply on the tile. In the living room, he flopped on the chair Bree had just vacated.

"How's the superjock doing these days?" he asked sarcastically, leaning his head back to pin Brianne with his lazy scrutiny.

Another time the look would have reduced her to a state of fluttering idiocy, but his casual dismissal of a man superior to him in character annoyed her.

"Neville is just fine," she said coolly. She crossed her arms and fixed *him* with a questioning look. "What can I do for you, Spence? I'm sure you have a reason for stopping by. And, how did you know I'd be here?"

He smiled slowly and patted the broad arm of the chair for her to join him.

"Oh, I had Gen—" He caught himself as a look of anger flashed across Bree's face. She raised her eyebrows.

"I might have known," she murmured. But it was only a brief twinge of hurt that troubled her. To their surprise, the ludicrousness of the situation nudged a chuckle from her. "And what did you have Gena do? It was under protest, I'm sure."

"That's not funny! I had her find out your schedule. When I called the press club and they said you weren't there and that Neville was, I figured I'd try here." He spoke quickly, trying to put distance between himself and his gaffe.

He smiled again ingratiatingly and patted the chair arm.

She shook her head, declining with a slow smile. The knowing look on her face made him uncomfortable. He rose and came to stand in front of her. By her reactions at the door and at the mention of Gena, he knew she still had some feeling left for him, but her calm in the face of his considerable charm suggested she might truly be slipping from his grasp.

"Bree," he lowered his voice intimately, caressing her shoulders with his hands. He tried then to slip his arms around her and pull her to him, but she put out her hands and held him off.

She stepped back a pace, dropping her eyes. She could tell she wasn't out of the woods of her affection for him yet. *Soon,* but not yet!

"Spence, you know I still—think a great deal of you. It's really no one's fault we broke up. I believe it was God's will because we just didn't share our faith in Christ—"

Spence threw his hands up in exasperation and spun

around. "We're back to that again!"

"Spence, if there's anything I can do to help you I will."

He turned and looked at her sharply. "You know, goody-two-shoes, I almost think you meant that." He came back and took her hands in his. For a rare moment he dropped the macho facade and was the serious, thoughtful man she knew he could be when he chose. But then he spoke again.

"There is a favor you could do for me. There's this dinner coming up at McBain's this weekend when they'll officially unveil the Manta. I'd really like to be there."

With a pang Bree knew he wouldn't go alone.

"Well, Spence," she looked doubtfully at him, "you know more about that than I do because it wasn't on *my* schedule—"

"For crying out—"

"Spence!" she cut him off. "I'll see what I can do about getting you in, okay?"

He held her gaze a moment longer. He knew he'd behaved badly, but apologies were foreign to his nature.

When she moved to the door in the foyer she heard his footsteps follow. He leaned over her shoulder and dropped a quick kiss on her cheek.

"Thanks Bree," he said sheepishly. "You've always been a good kid."

The phone rang as she was opening the door for him, giving him the excuse he needed to hurry away. She was just as glad he wasn't there to see her wipe away tears of disappointment and remorse for what could never have been.

The insistent ringing of the phone jarred her out of her melancholy reverie. She sniffed and hurried to the kitchen to pick up the receiver.

"It took you long enough!"

She smiled at the chipper voice. He'd come out of

his doldrums quickly, as if they'd never happened.

"Neville!" she said more warmly than she'd intended. She should have known better. He picked up on it immediately.

"What's wrong, Nanny? You sound bedeviled by something—or someone. What's transpired since I saw you this morning?"

"Nothing important," she hedged, but inside she glowed with the warmth of his concern.

"You wouldn't be trying to put me off."

"Yes, I would!" she laughed unsteadily, "but I'd rather not talk about it now, if you please. Or even if you don't please!"

"That's better. But keep in mind what I told you Monday night...."

She hadn't forgotten that he'd offered her a shoulder to cry on.

"Now, on to business!" he said. "It seems Mickey has added a black-tie dinner to our schedule, my dear, prior to the official unveiling of the Manta Saturday. Do you think you can outfit yourself on such short notice and accompany me? That is, if you don't mind a role reversal of being escorted?"

The request caught her off guard. Memory of last night at the lake returned. Well, at such a formal affair there would be no chance to set herself up for emotions she couldn't handle. It sounded safe enough.

"Hello? Are you still there?" She marveled. She could *hear* a difference in his voice when his mouth twisted in a grin. "Don't tell me you've finally come up against a situation you can't handle!"

"Ah—no. I was just thinking..." she stalled. "Let me go see what I've got in the closet. I think I have something that might do—" She started to lay the phone down only to grab it up again and tell him breathlessly, "Hang on!"

She didn't hear him laugh as she scampered off to the bedroom and threw open the closet door. She

87

rummaged frantically through the contents, the item she sought eluding her.

"Come on, I *know* you're here!" she snarled, poking the clothes to and fro impatiently. Karen goes to exclusive places a lot—could she have?—no. Bree's clothes were too big for her petite cousin. "Aha!" She grabbed the green satin hanger and drew out the gown with a silken slither. It fluttered before her as she hurried back to the phone.

"Well?" he prompted, hearing her pick up the receiver.

"You're in luck, Mr. Ross."

"Excellent! And by the way I've already seen to arranging for the regulation tuxedo. Do you think you might pick it up for me tomorrow?—oh yes! One more thing. What color might we be wearing if I may ask?"

"Red," she replied gaily. Just speaking with him had dispelled her bleak mood.

"Marvelous!" he cried. "Just what I'd hoped."

She reminded him of his evening obligations, but he explained he'd seen to them. Since he didn't say how, she thought she had one more pickup and delivery of his person in Birmingham that evening.

With a good bit of pique she arrived at his hotel that evening to find he'd checked out.

"Neville, I could wring your neck!" she exploded, turning her back on the curious desk clerk. "Now, how can I ferry you around if I don't even know where you are?"

"—Ma'am?" The desk clerk tapped her shoulder. She turned to him, scowling. "Mr. Ross left this for you."

She took the address, hastily scribbled on a piece of paper torn from his schedule, and thanked the clerk.

After getting turned around once or twice on Woodward north of Maple and stopping for directions at a service station, she was startled when she finally arrived at the address. It was the same house—at least she thought it was the same though it looked a little different in the light—that Neville had been staring at the night before, one of the ranches facing the lake. Turning into the drive she noticed it was empty. How had he gotten here? Better yet, why had he left the hotel and moved to this house? Given the brevity of his stay, it seemed rather pointless.

She walked the flagged path across the broad lawn to the door, her mind churning with questions. Tall windows looking out over the lake vista were open, their sheers lifting lazily on the breeze. There seemed to be no one within, no activity as she passed, but when she banged the heavy brass knocker she heard the sound of someone playing the piano. At first she thought it was the radio. Odd, she didn't think Neville was the type to like classical music. Well, what type did he seem?

Moot point, she conceded and knocked again louder.

The music stopped. Unreasoning fear seized her, along with a wild thought. What if he weren't alone? What if he had someone—a female someone...Her stomach did an odd flip-flop and she turned, contemplating flight.

"So you've finally found me! Well done!" He greeted her—alone—seeming to fill the golden oak frame of the heavy paneled door. "Come in, come in! I've just been relaxing with a bit of music. It calms the savage beast you know...."

"I think the word is *'breast,'* " she corrected absently.

"Whatever!" He seemed genuinely pleased to see her. Apparently so far the day had gone well.

"Music?" she stopped short in the marble-floored foyer. He closed the door behind her. "Was that—that wasn't *you* playing—was it?"

"That *bad,* eh? I don't know if I should admit to it then."

89

"No! I mean—it was very good!" She hurried on to correct herself and saw he was teasing her again. Except for the light mahogany grand piano before the curving bank of windows she'd passed, now on her right, the rooms were empty. There were a few large floor pillows arranged in front of the empty oak-paneled fireplace to the left. A book lying open by the pillows and a box of animal crackers suggested he'd been reading earlier.

The area to the left seemed to be the dining-entertainment area. Through the door in the distant rear wall she caught a glimpse of mellow-gold wood kitchen cabinets in a spacious kitchen. The living room where the piano sat was plastered and painted, but across the broad open expanse of the front of the house, the dining area was oak-paneled. Plush champagne beige carpeting ran throughout, but there was no other furniture to be seen.

There was also no light. In the August twilight the digital readout on her watch flashed 7:30, but the sunlight outside only penetrated the area around the piano. Two long windows on either side of the fireplace remained closed and draped. Two fat candles in heavy brass holders atop the mantel provided the only light on this side of the room. He'd been reading by candlelight?

"I forgot to have them turn on the electricity," he informed her. "My friend's in real estate; this is one of his houses. He lent me the keys for the rest of my stay so I could tinker around on the piano."

"Then you do play!" She regarded him with awe. How incongruous, a rough and tumble athlete who could—and liked to—play the piano.

He laughed at her expression.

"Yes, Mum had this crazy idea of making a concert pianist of me at one time, before football fever struck."

"It was nice of your friend to furnish the place..."

"The furniture's in storage. The owner left the

whole thing for Gerry to dispose of when he moved back to Europe."

Bree moved slowly along the curve of the piano's case, her fingers gliding over the satiny wood.

"I always wanted to learn how to play the piano," she mused. "Why don't you play something for me?" She turned with a coaxing smile.

"Name your tune," he invited, resuming his seat on the bench.

He diddled around a little, then played a Brahms waltz. She congratulated herself on recognizing it when he confirmed her guess with a nod. Then he moved into something more tempestuous. His hands moved swiftly back and forth from one side of the keyboard to the other, creating the underlying theme beneath the melody. When the passage calmed to a quieter part, Bree recognized the tune as one from a popular song from her mother's era.

"Chopin," he said to her questioning look. He was showing off for her, but she loved it.

He concluded the piece. "Now!" he said again, "name your tune."

"I'm thinking!" she laughed softly when he raised his eyebrows.

She glanced toward the lake. The moon was just visible above it in the twilight sky.

"How about Beethoven—the 'Moonlight Sonata'?" she suggested. It was her favorite piano piece.

He looked up again with a teasing grin. "I take it you mean the 'Adagio'?"

"I think that's the one," Bree nodded, and leaned back in delicious anticipation as he began to play.

Amazing that such big hands could traverse the board and coax such delicate nuances from the instrument. Her eyes followed his confident fingers over the keys.

He glanced up and smiled absently, absorbed by the sound he was creating. Her eyes roamed from his

hands to his long tanned forearms, the sunlight making a golden sheen of the hair covering them. Fascinated, she watched the play of muscle and tendon
beneath the taut surface of his skin. She let her gaze
wander up over the hard muscle of his upper arms and
shoulders, taking in the pale blue V-necked pullover
that just skimmed the surface of his chest. It was the
first time she'd really noticed that his neck was well-
shaped, not thick and muscular like those of a lot of
athletes his size.

Her eyes finally came to rest on his face, intent on
the music. He closed his eyes, leaning forward slightly,
completely entranced. Apparently it was one of his favorite sonatas, too. His sun-streaked hair fell forward
on his forehead. With her eyes Bree touched every
curve of his face, from the dark, downswept lashes
veiling his eyes to the clean line of his jaw and the
curving fullness of his lips.

The sudden rush of emotion she felt for him startled
her. No! She couldn't—she *wouldn't* let it be love! She
absolutely refused. It was ridiculous even to think it
could be. She stirred restlessly, shaken by her
thoughts. He looked up, raised a brow in question.
She shook her head indicating it was nothing and
moved like a sleepwalker to the open casement window. Leaning her back against the jamb, she turned to
watch him again and marveled anew. He really was
very good.

The melancholy music flowed up from under his
fingers to surround her and carry her away. She felt it
lift her out of herself till she was floating—drifting
above the lake, rising high enough to touch the pale
three-quarter moon just beginning to shine.

Smiling to herself, she watched the scenes on the
bank of the lake. A family with two small children
were feeding the swans. Their noisy delight changed
to uncertain alarm when one of the great birds leaned
a graceful neck forward to nibble a bread crust from

tiny fingers. A younger couple watching from the split rail fence around the park encouraged the children not to be afraid.

Neville watched her covertly. He caught her eye once or twice and smiled, but she was intent on the people by the lake, caught up in the brooding sadness of the music.

When an elderly couple strolled by hand in hand, their heads together enjoying the secrets of a long, shared life, her mind jumped to thoughts of Spence and her broken romance. Thoughts of what might have been assailed her. She felt a great sadness remembering the good side of himself that he suppressed in his rush to get ahead in the world. She wondered if she'd failed him in some way.

Come on, Tyler! She tried to shake the mood, but it persisted stubbornly. She felt the sting of tears, and before she could turn her face from Neville's view, one escaped and slid down her cheek. She hoped he hadn't seen.

The dampness of the mist rising from the lake finally reached the house. It touched her face, borne on the soft wind stirring through the cedars. The aromatic smell of the evergreens was drifting to her, earthy and sweet, when she suddenly heard silence. The music had stopped.

She looked up abruptly to find Neville standing before her. Her eyes opened wide with alarm, and her treacherous heart hammered out of control as she looked up at him. She wondered miserably how much he had seen, and she watched, unable to move, as he raised his hands to take her face in them as he had the night before.

His thumbs moved caressingly over her cheeks, the fingers seeking the fullness of the long hair around her neck, but it was the look in his eyes that held her. She made a half-hearted attempt to pull her head away from the scrutiny of his eyes but found it impossible.

93

"Brianne," he whispered hoarsely, lowering his face to hers, "Brianne, darling! Don't ever try to hide from me!"

His mouth brushed lightly across hers, then fluttered to her cheeks, her temples, her eyelids. Then, as his beautiful, curving lips returned to her trembling ones, they took possession. One hard arm slipped down around her to pin her tightly to him, his kiss becoming deeper, more demanding. She reeled against him and her arms slid up to encircle his neck, giving herself entirely to the feelings that had threatened her all week.

He released her and stepped back. Before she knew what he intended, he'd swept her up in his arms to carry her across the room. She buried her telltale face in the hollow of his neck and shoulder as he gripped her to him.

Disjointed thoughts skittered across the surface of Bree's mind like a flat pebble across a pond. *You have to stop this, Tyler! You're getting in too deep!* But how? She felt powerless, at the mercy of her churning emotions. The strength of her reaction to him left her stunned.

He lowered her onto the big pillows, bracing one behind her, and reclined beside her, one arm under her head. She couldn't hide her feelings from him now as he looked down into her eyes. They were all there, open to his acute perception. Gently he traced the line of her brow, her cheek, down along her jaw. He didn't speak but followed with his lips the path his finger traced over her face, till he reached her neck. His breathing grew rough and uneven.

She felt as well as saw in his eyes his desire for her. Unwittingly her fingers twisted in his thick hair as his lips moved down her neck to the soft hollow at its base. His hand on her back turned her toward him more. His mouth burned on the pulsing skin of her throat.

"No!" she sobbed in protest. It couldn't be love! She'd loved Spence, but she had never experienced anything of this magnitude with him. She cared enough for Neville to want to yield to his gentle leading. He was more of a danger to her than Spence had ever been. She had to get out! For the sake of her faith and her self-respect, she had to get away from him!

She was crying uncontrollably now.

"What—" Neville gasped as she pushed away from him and broke out of his hold. Before he could react, she had jumped to her feet and run to the piano. Grabbing her purse, she turned and fled to the door. She heard him behind her, stumbling to his feet, hurt and confusion in his voice.

"Brianne! Brianne, wait!"

She had to get away! Escape was the only thought on her mind now. She didn't want him to see how much she cared. Stupid! How could she care? She'd just been in love with Spence. What kind of person was she?

Blinded by the tears and reproach burning through her brain, she threw open the heavy door and ran down the steps, propelled forward by the fear of being caught. Her car seemed a mile from the house.

"Brianne, for Pete's sake! Tell me what I've done?" He was coming after her. She panicked. With his long legs, he'd overtake her easily!

She ran faster, slamming into the car and fumbling for the handle.

"Brianne!" he shouted angrily.

It struck her for a moment what a strange scene *they* must be presenting to the people across the street in the park.

She heard him running across the grass. The car door was locked! Of all times for her to have been cautious! "Oh, no!" she groaned, tearing open her purse in frustration. Luckily, she found the key quickly, grabbed it, unlocked the door, and was ready to jump in when she heard Neville fall. He went down heavily and moaned.

Was he faking, trying to trick her into coming back to check on him? She turned, hesitating. He lay on the ground clutching his right knee—the bad one. She took a few tentative steps toward him.

His head was stretched back, eyes closed, face taut in pain. He wasn't faking.

She ran to him quickly.

"What's wrong—what is it?" she asked, dropping to her knees beside him in the grass.

"This blasted soccer knee," he tried to laugh, but he caught his breath, his face twisting in agony. "Mind your dress," he said between clenched teeth, opening one eye to look at her.

"Forget the stupid dress! Let's get you back inside and have a look at that knee, see if you've damaged anything irreparably!"

"Probably not." He allowed her to help him to his feet, one arm braced across her shoulders, the other around his waist for support as she helped him back to the house.

With a quick flick of his eyes toward the people watching from the lake side, he whispered above Bree's ear, "You can go home now, folks—the main event of the evening is over!"

Blood rushed to Bree's face in embarrassment.

"Why are *you* sticking around?" he asked her. "Afraid you'll lose your job by returning a gimpy star to the boss tomorrow?"

She shot him a look of alarm.

He grinned wanly in apology and hugged her with the arm resting on her shoulders.

"It *is* your fault, you know," he added, but by this time she knew he was nudging her for another reaction.

"Yes, I know," she replied anyway, guilt in her voice. "I never should have let it go that far."

"Nonsense!" He stopped abruptly, hobbling around to face her.

"Brianne Tyler..." He noticed the people across the street still watching and jerked his head toward the door. "Come in here and tell me all about it. I think you owe me that much."

She passed through the door for the second time that night, and he closed it with a loud click behind her.

Chapter Eight

Brianne guided Neville to the pillows before the fireplace, settling him on one and propping up his knee. She banked another behind him, then kneeled down on the floor.

"Okay, let's see it." She flicked a hand at the knee.

"Really, it'll be fine," he protested with a sheepish grin.

"—unless there's really nothing wrong after all," she suggested with a pointed look and made as if to rise. She knew he'd hurt it. But to what extent? That was a different question. Enough to keep her here?

"No, wait." He grabbed her arms and pulled her back down beside him, then slowly rolled back the beige linen trouser leg to expose the knee. The surgical scars ran like angry red tracks across the skin. Even the soft light of the two candles didn't mitigate the effect.

She looked up quickly.

"Oh, it doesn't hurt—anymore," he hastened to assure her, "except psychologically! I just turn wrong sometimes and the blasted thing goes out on me."

She leaned back to rest on her heels. Misinterpreting the move as another attempt to leave, he seized her arms again.

"Don't go!"

Something in the way he said it and the imploring look in his eyes made her sit still, watching him thoughtfully for an instant. He confused her. His eyes said one thing, his lips another. Was he only indulging in a serious flirtation, or was he in fact serious?

She sighed, breaking the tension.

"I wasn't going to leave," she said. He was right about one thing. She did owe him an explanation for her own contradictory behavior.

"Tell me what happened just now. I thought that you were—that you wanted me as much as I wanted you." Feelings warred behind his eyes. He was couching his words cautiously and she wondered why. Was he afraid of revealing too little, or too much?

But the subject had been broached. *Here it is,* she sighed heavily. Where to begin? How to explain to him the higher authority that guided her behavior?

"I'm not the sort of man who indulges himself with every pretty face he comes across if that's what you were thinking, Brianne," he said more seriously than she'd known him to speak yet. "Is that what you thought?"

He took her chin and raised her face so she was forced to look in his eyes. There was no laughter in them now.

"Not exactly." She tried to lower her eyes, but he shook her chin gently.

"I like to see your eyes when you're talking to me," he said. "Those big, dark eyes are like pools of hot fudge sauce."

She laughed despite the angry retort that came to mind—*so you can read my mind without letting me see what you feel?* But she said instead, "Always thinking of your stomach!"

"Oh," he chuckled, seeing the flash in her eyes before she spoke, "that makes you mad, does it?"

Was she supposed to guess from the way he looked

100

at her that he felt the same as she did? Well, looks didn't count—words did.

"You didn't answer my question, dear. Do you think I'm the sort to play fast and loose?"

"No, I don't think so. But then I don't really know. We hardly know one another, do we?"

"True enough." She could tell by the way his irises widened he'd meant to say something else but changed his mind. "But I think we've been in one another's company long enough to get some definite character readings, don't you?"

"I suppose."

"I'd hoped you'd feel you could trust me. Oh," he sighed with self-directed annoyance, "I know I've teased the dickens out of you, but when you started at Metro Monday with your little 'I've got everything under control here, Bucko!' business, I couldn't help it. You practically invited a takedown!"

She winced at that, nearly laughing again at his accurate reading of her attitude four days ago, but she kept her face straight and countered, "Apparently you need someone in charge—to keep you on schedule, *Bucko!*"

"Your goal!" he noted, grinning broadly. "But we're getting away from the question at hand. *Why* did you run away? I know you were experiencing the same...." He stopped, searching for the right words. The look she'd seen in his eyes before she broke away from his embrace earlier came into them again, and he started to draw her to him.

She quickly put her hands out to grip his arms, holding him back.

"Yes, I was. The truth is, the feelings scared me. I've never felt that way before...." She paused and felt the blood rush to her face. Anger with herself for blushing supplanted her confusion.

"There now," he soothed, raising one hand to stroke her face. "I should have guessed you weren't as so-

101

phisticated as you tried to appear—as cool and—'in charge'!"

"Please don't treat me like a child. I'm not, though I know I act like it sometimes. I have my reasons for not getting physically—involved with you, or any man, outside of marriage, no matter how much I might have wanted to."

Unknowingly she had answered his question, but she didn't notice the anxious tension line between his eyebrows ease up.

Here goes! she thought, determined to stick to her promise to her Lord, no matter the outcome. Her determination calmed her turbulent emotions, and she chose her words carefully, still anxious about alienating him.

"As a Christian I believe that physical intimacy is a gift from God, meant to be shared over a lifetime, in marriage. It's not something to be tossed about casually and indiscriminately."

"I do *not* toss myself about casually or indiscriminately!"

"No, I don't think you do. But it's not something I can take lightly, no matter how much I—" she caught herself and looked up quickly, but she should have known it wouldn't slip by his notice.

"So it frightened you, did it?" His eyes were like blue fire burning through her. "Are you telling me the erstwhile Spencer Kenyon never inspired such passion from you?"

"No..."

"Good," he said with a smug smile, crossing his arms across his chest and settling against the pillows.

"No, it *isn't* good, Neville Ross, and stop distracting me!" she said, exasperatedly tapping his arm with the back of her hand. He grabbed the hand and held it captive between his own.

"Brianne, if things had gone on in their natural direction a few minutes ago, I can assure you my intent was no light, casual fling."

"It doesn't matter."

"But, I'd still have respected and—liked—you." There it was again, the slight hesitation as if he had substituted another word for the one he intended. He was holding back.

But Bree was too involved with her own thoughts to give it much notice. "That's what I'm trying to tell you! *I* wouldn't have liked me if I'd gone along with it. I would have hurt myself and not only me but someone I love dearly, my Lord."

"Well surely He wouldn't chuck you out of the fold for *one* mistake!"

"No, it's not that. He'd still love me, but I would have let both of us down. He's given clear guidance in the Bible and I know what it is. To go against that deliberately..."

"Let *God* down? I wouldn't think He expected much from us in the first place. After all, isn't that why He's God, and we're human, so He can save us from our mistakes?"

At first she thought he was humoring her, and she couldn't decide whether that or Spence's outright mockery was worse. Then she picked up overtones of an unspoken resentment in his interrogation, an underlying bitterness toward the Lord.

Be that as it may, she knew where her responsibility lay.

"I've learned what's right and what's wrong," she said softly, "and even without God's word to tell me I would have felt it was wrong. Besides, I promised earlier this week that I would never again get involved with a man who doesn't believe as I do, with whom I can't share everything important in my life—including faith in Christ."

"I've learned the hard way the meaning of a particular principle, 'Be ye not unequally yoked with unbe-

103

lievers', because the things that I value don't mean the same to someone else..."

"And where is this principle found?" he asked. "It sounds disturbingly familiar."

"It's in the second epistle to the Corinthians, chapter six, verse fourteen," she said with a curious look at him. He was familiar with the passage?

But she'd said her piece, calmly and dispassionately, she hoped. He could do with it what he wished.

To her surprise he did nothing at first, just held her hand and stared pensively at some point across the room behind her. Then his brow creased in a frown.

"I used to believe God cared about me," he said. He shook off the expression and fastened sharp eyes on her again. "Was that your problem with Kenyon?"

"I thought at first that...well... Spence made fun of me for believing."

He made a sound of disgust. "To be sure! Finesse is not his long suit." He held up a hand to stop her reply. "I will not listen to you try to defend that—that—"

Leaning forward he swept her in his arms again, pulling her head down on his chest as he eased back against the pillow. His left hand wrapped itself in her hair which she was sure was hopelessly tangled by now.

"Brianne, no matter what might have happened or *will* happen, you'll never do anything to make me dislike or disrespect you. I value your—friendship—too much!"

They were both holding back. They were on the edge of a greater emotional commitment than Bree had ever known. And while *she* refused to give in to it without a fight, she wondered why *he* was so cautious.

They sat together for what seemed a long time, the steady rise and fall of his chest under her head nearly lulling her to sleep. When she finally stirred and sat back up, he let her go with reluctance.

"Will you be all right?" she asked with an anxious

look at his knee and its ominous scars.

"Yes," he laughed ruefully. "It'll be all better in the morning—well enough to go a few games with Mickey on the racquetball court!"

"Racquetball! You've got to be kidding."

"Oh, no! Mickey doesn't kid around!"

She shook her head and rose to her feet.

"I really have to get going. You're *sure* you don't need to have a doctor look at your knee?"

"Give me a hand up, love." He reached out a hand to her, balancing himself with the other and his good leg as he tottered to his feet. When she put her arms around his waist to steady him, he crushed her to him again, looking down at her with his eyes half-closed.

"Behave," she warned.

"Yes, Nanny." He released her, flicking the tip of her nose with his finger. He limped to the door leaning on her shoulder. "There's a jacuzzi in the hot tub out back. I'll have a soak in that for a while, and the knee should be fine."

"A hot tub *and* a jacuzzi? Be careful you don't fall asleep while you're soaking. I'd hate to pick up the morning paper and read 'Ex-Soccer Star Bubbled to Death in Runaway Jacuzzi!' "

"If you're that concerned you could stay and oversee the operation."

She ignored his comment and opened the front door. He leaned on the frame to ease the weight off his bad knee.

"Oh!" She clapped a hand over her mouth in consternation, remembering a promise she'd made that afternoon. In a spirit of mischief to match his own, she decided now was as good a time as any to present it.

"What is it?"

"There's a favor I have to ask—for a friend. And since you seem to have Mr. McBain's ear..."

"Just name it!" he invited unsuspectingly.

"Do you think you could possibly get a dinner invitation for Saturday's unveiling for Spen—"

"Brianne!" Fury flared in his eyes, but only for a moment. "You little minx," he grinned, taking her hand.

"I promised I'd ask, and I did ask! Now, good night, *Mr.* Ross."

"Good night, Brianne." He leaned over to kiss her lightly, inviting a response. She pulled away reluctantly.

"You're *sure* you don't need to see a—"

"I'll be *fine!* Now run along! We have to be at the club at seven!"

She waved to his silhouetted form in the doorway after backing down the long drive to the street. In the rearview mirror she watched him as long as she could till a bend in the road cut off her view. The faint aroma of his scent where his skin had touched hers lingered as a bittersweet reminder of the evening, and it occurred to her that her game had gotten wildly out of hand. Neville, the cure, was more disastrous than Spence, the cause of her distress.

Neville. What exactly did he feel toward her? She caught her breath without realizing it. He'd evoked a flood of response from her tonight that she hadn't even known she possessed. She still balked at calling it love. She went cold with the thought. Whatever it was, it was more than she'd ever felt for Spence, and, strangely, that made her feel guilty.

Stop it, Tyler! Spence had chosen the course he wanted to pursue. She put him out of her mind. She didn't want to think about him anyway. Monday seemed like a century away now.

Neville. In her mind she saw his face when she'd told him where she stood. She believed he meant it when he said she could do nothing to make him dislike her. He'd listened—actually *listened*—when she'd explained her reasons for avoiding physical intimacy with him, without getting angry, swearing, or storming out. Not that he would have been able to storm out without her help!

No man could do or say those things unless he really cared. Or look at her the way he had. So why was he holding back? Did talking about her commitment to Christ put him off? She didn't think so. What was it he'd said—*I used to believe that once...* She tried to remember his exact words, but they eluded her. No matter. She knew why she was holding back, and with so much riding on the outcome, she was more determined than ever to keep her promise.

Neville stood in the door watching the red slits of the Camaro's taillights till they disappeared behind a copse at the road's curve. Then he closed the heavy door and hobbled across the house to the back deck. The knee was sore enough, but not as bad as he had led Brianne to believe.

He chuckled warmly at the thought of her and shook his head. *What am I to do with you, Brianne. Better still, what have you done to me?*

Halfway to the jacuzzi, he changed his mind. Doing an about-face he returned to the bedroom. He rummaged through neat stacks of clothes around his suitcase on the bed and finally found what he was looking for. He unearthed the battered blue box and opened it.

"Maybe this is why I've dragged you around with me all these years," he murmured, tipping the box to let a burgundy morocco-bound Bible fall into his hand. He ran a finger over the lettering on the cover and flicked it open to the flyleaf.

"To Neville, from Mother and Dad," read the inscription. "June 19, 1962—'If any man be in Christ, he is a new creature. Old things are passed away. Behold, all things are become new.'"

"All things are become new," he repeated. After a moment he added, with a crooked self-mocking smile, "You know—you just might win this time."

Chapter Nine

"Are you *sure* your knee will stand the pounding?"

"Yes!" Neville jerked his tan flannel trouser leg up to reveal a heavy brace. "Are you satisfied now, Nanny?"

She made a face at him.

"That'll keep it from going out on me, and besides, I doubt that after thirty-six holes of golf yesterday Mickey will be much of a threat on the court anyway. Golf's his game, not racquetball. Since Nell outfitted him in racket, suit, and accessories for his birthday he feels obligated to play."

Following Neville's directions, Brianne headed the Camaro along the tree-lined road curving up to Oakhill Country Club. Tall willows, their graceful, trailing branches sweeping almost to the ground, stood before tall old cedars screening the clubhouse from the main road. To the left of the sprawling red brick clubhouse, the green of the golf course rolled down to meet a small lake surrounded by maples and more willows, the bane of many a golfer who used the course.

Brianne smiled, stealing a covert look at Neville. He hadn't mentioned last night or their discussion, but the situation between them had changed for him as well as herself. There was an air of the intimacy that comes with the deepening of a friendship when discussing even the mundane business of life.

In a way she felt disappointed that he hadn't said anything.

What did you expect him to say? she thought. "*I really enjoyed chasing you and hurting my knee when you ran away last night*"? *Time to get things back in control! It's business, Tyler, remember?* But somehow that reminder didn't have the same force anymore.

"Why so silent?" he asked. She knew he'd been watching her again, and she found the observation unnerving.

He traced the line of her brow and cheek with a hand, sweeping her hair back from her face. Despite her intention not to, she turned and smiled.

"Sometimes, *Ms.* Tyler, you are entirely too grave and it's those times you arouse in me the overwhelming desire to tickle you without mercy."

"I knew it. Your outrageousness is only to provoke a reaction," she accused lightly. Why did she wish he would say something about last night?

"No, it's only to keep your attention on me," he replied. "I get jealous of anyone or anything that claims such intense concentration from you."

Here was an opening. But she lost her nerve. Common sense dictated a change of subject.

"I was just regretting that I didn't bring a book to read while you and Mr. McBain chase around on the court."

"I have a better idea. Why don't you have breakfast while Mickey and I have at it?" He looked at his watch. "It's just seven now. You can't have had time to eat before fetching me."

"No," she admitted, "and now that you've brought the subject up, I'm afraid my stomach won't let me forget it either!"

"Good! Pull in there—I believe the courts and locker rooms are just inside that entrance." He pointed out a spot at the right wing of the clubhouse. "I would be very surprised if we haven't arrived before our host. It looks like Martell's group is already setting up, too."

Bree recognized the big equipment and camera trucks on one side of the lot, with the trailer dressing room. The men were busily hauling out equipment for filming in front of the country club. The trailer with the Manta under a tight-fitting cover sat a little way off, with Bruce and the propmaster on guard nearby.

Neville jumped out of the car after a crew member had checked them through the roped-off lot and they'd parked. Hauling his gym bag from the back seat while Bree was still setting the parking brake, he raced around to her door.

"Don't you dare!" he warned as she reached for the handle to let herself out. Slinging the bag over his shoulder, he helped her out. "I have a reputation to maintain around here!"

She laughed, thrilling at his nearness when he rested an arm lightly around her for the walk to the building entrance.

Oh, Tyler! Why do you court disaster so? she thought.

"Good morning, Ross." The words, cold and bitten off, brought them up short as Spence stepped out of the locker room to confront them. Apparently he'd been watching for them.

"Kenyon," Neville drawled, extending his hand slowly.

"I guess you're surprised to see me, Ross," Spence challenged, taking a stand squarely before them.

He was dressed in a snappy shorts and shirt ensemble, with matching head and wristbands, and had a racquetball racket in his hands. Surely McBain hadn't invited him to play as well?

"I guess I am," Neville replied coolly with an infuriatingly cordial smile.

111

"McBain had an emergency call from the film company. He asked me to fill in for him." Spence took the proffered hand with reluctance as the two men squared off.

"Well. I assume by your outfit you're an avid follower of the sport?"

Bree looked uneasily at the two men. The animosity between them was almost tangible.

"I've played quite a bit," Spence said with smug modesty. Bree knew he wasn't interested in sports, outside of Monday night football or an occasional Tigers or Pistons game, but he took his racquetball seriously. Charlie Bates had complained more than once about his murderous intensity during lunchtime games at the court near the Tech. She watched Spence covertly size Neville up, counting on the difference in their sizes to be in his favor.

"Since we both have a full day ahead of us, perhaps we should get at it, right?" Neville glanced in the direction Spence had come from. "Locker rooms are this way—?"

"Yeah," Spence nodded shortly. "Bree and I can wait for you here."

"Brianne, why don't you go ahead to the dining room, and I'll meet you there after the game," Neville suggested instead. There was a polite question in his eyes. She knew he was offering her an escape from this encounter with Spence, and her gratitude for his concern showed. Spence looked quickly from Neville to her, anger flickering in his gaze.

"You've monopolized Brianne this entire week, so we have a lot to catch up on, Ross."

Neville looked at Bree, raising his eyebrows, but Bree sent him off with an imperceptible nod. He glanced back once, she noted happily, just before disappearing through the locker room door. Then she was alone with Spence.

She'd thought reason, time, the distraction of

Neville and his new importance in her affections had buffered her from Spence. But she caught full force the flashing anger in his eyes as he turned on her.

"That was such a pretty little speech you made yesterday," he began coolly enough, but she knew he was working up to a towering harangue. " 'Spence, if there's anything I can do to help you I will!' "

So Neville had already talked to McBain and Spence wouldn't be present at the unveiling.

"Spence, I tried—"

"Did you really!" His face contorted with anger. " 'I—bear you no ill will' huh? Miss Goody-Two-Shoes? Baloney! You can save the all-forgiving act for the superjock! Keeping me on the outside with him—and now with McBain—is just your way of paying me back for breaking up with you!"

Bree was stunned. She marveled that rage could make such a fine, handsome face so ugly—so hard and cruel-looking. His lips were drawn back over his teeth, the lines beside his nose deepened to harsh slashes.

Looking at him now and comparing him to her first impressions of him was like watching a beautiful dream turn into an out-of-control nightmare.

"You really could have helped me by putting in a good word with Ross, if you aren't all you pretend to be!" He punctuated his words with jabbing motions of the racket. "No, you had to play your little game, encouraging Ross to get back at me—make me jealous! If he weren't such a dumb, bumbling jock, he'd have seen what you were up to that first night at McBain's!"

"That's enough, Spence!" She broke into his tirade, trembling with fury. It hurt that he'd turned out so different from who she thought he was, but it also startled her that he'd seen through her little game with Neville.

"No, I'm not through yet, Brianne."

She cast a frightened glance toward the locker room.

Spence's voice carried. What if Neville had heard that last accusation?

"There's also the matter of—"

"I don't want to hear any more of this, Spence!" She said it with finality and turned her back on him striding off purposefully in the direction of the dining room.

So that's the game we've been playing, my dear!
Neville watched Brianne's stiff back as she retreated from the confrontation with Spence. *Kenyon, you cur!*

Noiselessly he came up behind Spence while he watched Bree disappear through the multipaned glass door of the dining room across the lobby.

"Afraid I'm going to be a poor match for you, Kenyon." Startled, Spence spun around to face him. Neville continued in a smooth apology. "Not only is this not my game, but I've wrenched this knee again and have to be careful of it." He drew Spence's interested gaze to his knee with a wave of Mickey's racket. The other man's eyes lit at sight of the reinforced elastic brace, a reaction not lost on Neville.

"I don't know, Ross—you're pretty sharp, on a soccer field," Spence demurred. "At least, you were till you got hurt. But that's a kind of skill you don't soon forget. You'll probably give me a good workout." He grinned slyly, turning to lead Neville to the court McBain had reserved.

"Like a lamb to the slaughter," Neville muttered under his breath. Kenyon apparently already considered the victory his.

"What?" Spence swiveled around with a suspicious look.

"I said this will probably be a slaughter," Neville repeated, strolling around the end of the court, favoring his knee. *At least I hope it will be,* he grinned to himself.

"How 'bout a few practice shots?" Spence called jovially, jogging around the perimeter to where Neville flexed his knees in tentative shallow bends.

"Fine. But don't expect too much. As I said, it's been a long time since I played."

"I'll go easy on you the first game," Spence laughed, licking his lips in anticipation. He poised, racket aloft.

Neville gave him a worried look. "Give it a go, mate."

Pock! The sound vibrated through the court as Spence's serve slammed off the back wall toward Neville.

Ka-Spock! Spence barely had time to scramble back across the court to catch Neville's high-powered return. He realized too late he'd forgotten to allow for the obvious strength in the long, muscular arms.

He fixed a suspicious eye on the Australian, watching with chagrin as time after time he effortlessly returned the ball by doing little more than knotting his muscles and extending his racket. Still, he was handicapped by the gimpy knee. Spence reasoned his own speed and agility would make up the difference between them.

Neville watched Spence's expression from the corner of his eye, waiting. Spence was racing back toward him, reaching for the ball with his racket, when it happened. His foot hit something solid and sent him sprawling across the court directly in front of Neville.

"Are you all right?" Neville stood over Spence, reached down to help him up, and jerked his 175-pound frame to his feet as if he weighed nothing. Then he fetched his racket from where it had landed against the wall. "That was a bad tumble. Are you sure you're all right? I'm terribly sorry. It was all my fault. These big feet of mine..."

"I'm fine! I'm fine!" Spence brushed himself off, grabbing the proffered racket. He rubbed the floor burn on his knee gingerly. "Just watch it, okay?"

"Sure thing, old man! Won't happen again!" Neville

was all solicitude that first time.

Neville was all solicitude and profuse apology each time after, as well. The time that Spence, going for a volley, slammed into Neville and bounced back onto the floor. The time Neville went after Spence's shot with a slow-motion run and stumbled into him. The time they both ran for the speeding blur of black ball and collided, Neville landing sprawled on top of Spence.

By his ineptitude, Neville won all three games. Using his knee as an excuse, he stood pretty much in one spot and ran Spence off his legs. Neville only seemed to move in order to trip, fall on, or run into Spence.

"Do we have time for another game?" Neville, barely winded, asked as he picked up the ball rolling back from the rear wall.

"No!" Spence gasped, wiping his streaming face with a towel. "I still—have to go in to the office today!" he panted. He turned on Neville, suspicion burning in his eyes. "I don't know how you did it, Ross—"

"Kenyon!" Neville cried taken aback. "It was *luck*, pure and simple! You're definitely the superior player, but you just had a run of bad breaks, what with my clumsiness today." He shook his head, looking puzzled.

Spence wasn't buying it. He grabbed up his racket from the floor and limped to the door.

"I enjoyed it, Kenyon! Perhaps we can do it again sometime—"

"No way!" Spence replied and hustled out the door.

"My word!" Bree greeted Spence in the hall a few minutes later. "If you're in such sad shape, what condition must Neville be in?"

"That's not funny, Bree!" Spence snapped, still mopping at wet tendrils of hair plastered on his forehead. He gave her a withering look, rubbing his shoul-

116

der. "I'm lucky I don't have any broken bones, no thanks to that oaf!"

Slinging his bag over his shoulder, he turned abruptly and headed for the exit. "He'll never set foot on the same racquetball court with me again!"

It wasn't meant to be funny, Bree mused, watching with a worried look as he stumbled wearily out the door.

The sound of someone whistling a jaunty tune drew her attention back to the court door. Neville sauntered out pulling a broken string on his racket. She hadn't seen him dressed for play. Unlike Spence, he was all in white—shorts, shirt, shoes and all. His tan had never seemed more golden.

Her eyes fastened on his knees with acute interest as he walked, especially the right one with the heavy brace. There was barely a trace of limp in his gait.

"Oh, hello!" He grinned in delight at seeing her. He ambled up and drew her to him with one arm for a sound kiss.

"Careful!" she gasped, pulling away flustered.

"Whyever?"

"I...ah...the management of this place might frown on such demonstrations."

"True, they are rather stuffy. But I'm not!"

"What went on in there? Spence looked as if he'd been horsewhipped."

"Why—racquetball, of course!"

"I take it you won?" She raised an eyebrow at him.

"Yes. So I did, so I did. Didn't realize how dreadfully out of shape I am—gave poor Kenyon the devil of a time, what with tripping over my own feet and all...."

She gave him a probing look.

"In spite of your bad knee—" She crossed her arms, waiting.

He smiled and shook his head.

"Amazing how rejuvenating those jacuzzis can be!"

The beeper alarm on his watch went off. "I'd better shower and change. Mickey will be here soon and they'll want me out front—" He shot an anxious glance toward the side door and sidled off to the locker room. "Don't go away—be back in a jif."

He turned and loped off to the locker room, no trace now of a limp in his gait.

Bree walked thoughtfully to a padded bench in the hall and sank on it to await his return. Her imagination freely played scenes of what might have happened on the court, and she fell back against the wall, convulsed with silent laughter.

"How'd the game go?" McBain bustled through the side door with a pair of self-important looking people in his wake.

"Very well, apparently," Bree said, unable to suppress a smile.

McBain stopped before her, hands on hips.

"Has our Neville been naughty? I arranged this match before I knew of his aversion to Kenyon—"

"Come now, Mickey." Neville, freshly showered and dressed, joined them. His hair clung in damp little points over his ears and above the open collar of his brown knit shirt. In his right hand he held the racket. "Sorry about this, Mickey," he held it out to McBain. "I'll have it restrung for you as soon as I can."

"Not to worry, son. It's a good excuse to put it away in the closet and hope Nell forgets it! Got carried away, did you?"

"Guess I don't know my own strength," Neville said, ignoring Bree's choked laughter.

"Don't bother to finish dressing, Neville. They're set up out there now, and the makeup artist is ready, so go straight to the trailer. This is it!"

Neville winced.

"Come on," he lowered his head and fixed Bree with a malevolent smile, "Don't think you can escape this ordeal by pretending to be *just* my driver." He

118

pulled her to her feet and outside with him to join the milling crowd of technicians and crew.

The same man who'd directed them in stills stood guard at the drive, directing curious club members to another parking lot. One of the big trucks and the trailer had been moved to the luxuriant lawn in front of the club house's Corinthian-pillared portico. Bree imagined the groundskeeper and head gardener must be having fits at all the feet trampling their handiwork.

"We had a change of plans," McBain was explaining. "We were unable to get the location we wanted, so we decided this was just as good. The main exteriors will be shot here. Then we'll finish the insert shots later." He stepped over black cables snaking from the camera car to a monitor just beyond and behind them. "That is, if everything works out." He and Neville exchanged rueful glances.

Several people were already standing around, waiting in evening dress and makeup. Bree felt sympathy for the models who had to wear furs and appear cool in the mounting morning heat. She was also aware of the admiring, covetous glances they gave her as she passed through the set with Neville. She felt herself flush with embarrassment as a couple of the models whispered and nodded in her direction. There was something more going on than the filming of a commercial, she suspected, feeling an expectant but mysterious undercurrent. She'd never thought about it before, but being the friend—especially a female friend—of a celebrity like Neville could be a problem.

Neville's grip suddenly tightened on her hand, crushing the bones together. She looked quickly at his face. His brows were drawn down in a frown. His face was taut and distant as it had been the night they'd driven out to the lake. He stared in the direction of the trailer with a worried question in his eyes.

"Jennifer arrived quite a while ago," McBain said shortly, and Bree felt excluded as some sort of secret empathy passed between the two men. "She's been giving makeup and wardrobe fits ever since."

"Amazing," Neville commented coldly. "She's on time for once in her life."

Bree thought it was a strange thing for him to say, and something in the way he spoke set off a warning in her mind as if she'd been dashed with cold water. How much, really, did she know about Neville Ross? Why did she suddenly sense approaching disaster?

For one thing, it had to do with her aching hand. She wriggled her fingers in his crushing grasp.

"Oh, my dear, forgive me!" Startled, he looked down at her and apologized. He raised the bruised hand and rubbed it between his own, the withdrawn look replaced by concern.

"Mr. Ross, you're wanted in wardrobe," one of the crew summoned him. He still lingered a minute beside her.

"Don't go yet, okay?" He turned to her, an undefinable worry in his eyes.

"Of course I'll stay," she assured him, ignoring the warning signals in her mind.

He drew a breath of relief and squeezed her hands before turning away to the trailer where a number of people were waiting for him. But he took a round-about route and disappeared behind some equipment.

Bree watched with fascination again as the set took shape. The Manta had been driven down from its trailer, uncovered, and rolled to one end of the club's long facade. The front entrance of the country club itself was to be the set for the fancy dress commercial. Its tall white columns and white shutters the height of the double-hung, multipaned windows made the building look more like something out of a Colonial Williamsburg brochure than an exclusive club in the middle west.

Models in tuxedos and exquisite evening gowns lounged around on the porch waiting for the shooting to begin. A couple of men rolled a long red carpet from inside the double doors of the entrance down across the two low steps and the drive.

The glass in the double doors and the windows sparkled. The Manta sparkled. Everything sparkled in the early morning light.

At a sudden commotion, Bree looked toward the trailer. People backed away as the door opened and she caught sight of a bit of blond fluff over their heads as Jennifer Thrale emerged to take her place on the set.

A cacophony preceded the crowd escorting Miss Thrale. People packed so closely around her, Bree could only catch glimpses of her bright hair, touches of white fur, and a flash of black.

"Come on, everybody, please!" Kurt Martell, hair wild as ever, confronted the knot of people and impatiently waved his arms. "Is this really necessary? Jennifer, can you have your people move off the set, please? Let Miss Thrale through there—over here, Jennifer dear..."

He stood poised to receive the delicate, perfectly manicured hand that emerged languidly from the crowd to alight on his. Bree nearly giggled at the expression on his face as he tried to hide his exasperation and register the proper mix of awe and enchantment.

Well, Bree couldn't deny that the woman was beautiful. The ubiquitous 'bones' were there, of course. Her face was well defined and delicately molded with high cheek bones, a narrow straight nose, and sensuous full lips.

Her heavily accented and outlined porcelain blue eyes brushed over Bree and dismissed her as no one of importance. The eyes continued to search the periphery for someone not yet present. Bored, she turned her attention to the director again as her private hairdresser sprayed down wisps of the profuse blond hair.

The beauty was there all right, on the surface. Not

even the harsh makeup necessary for filming could destroy the natural loveliness beneath, but somehow it was cold and distant.

Jennifer fidgeted beside the Manta, her fur wrap slipping to give more than a glimpse of her gown. Black on one side and white on the other it flashed sequined spangles with her every movement. The long-sleeved black half was slashed daringly across the front to a point at her waist on the right. The right side was white and sleeveless and was beaded like hoarfrost on a window. Tight-fitting at the waist, the dress flowed in controlled folds to just above the knee where black and white parted in a slit to display Jennifer's legs and tiny ankles, well-known from her stocking ads.

Bree looked away. She couldn't take much more visual perfection.

"Well—I'm no Jennifer Thrale, but will I do?" Neville joined her quietly while the fuss over his counterpart continued. He'd changed to a tux with black satin cummerbund, bow tie, wing collar, and onyx shirt studs. His hair was styled like a TV newscaster's and sprayed stiff.

She felt her lips twitch betrayingly and ducked her head, but not fast enough.

"Please, try to control yourself," he murmured. But even with laughter glinting in his eyes, he seemed nervous and glanced uneasily toward the set once or twice. "Brianne—" the urgency in his tone made her look up again. She'd never seen him so serious, and even more unusual for him, uncertain. "Brianne, I want you to do me a favor."

"Of course," she said promptly, alarmed at the change in him, "anything! What's wrong?"

"Nothing to worry about," he assured her. He gripped her shoulders lightly and looked into her eyes. "Just stand here where I can see you, okay?" His eyes probed hers. She trembled within, remembering the night before when he'd looked at her the same way.

But this time he seemed to be looking for understanding from her, instead of giving it. *Understanding for what?* she wondered.

"Neville!"

She felt a tiny tremor run through him at Jennifer's gleeful greeting. He grimaced at Bree and turned to go.

"No escape now!" he muttered inexplicably and pointed at Bree. "Remember—*stay here!*"

"Neville, darling!" Jennifer's boredom vanished. Hangers-on backed away as she made for Neville with outstretched arms. "Oh—my makeup!" she remembered and drew back again. "*Do* take those hands out of your *pockets!*" she ordered.

It was playfully done—but it *was* a command. She prodded him with a hand, then twined both arms around his left arm and held on.

"Yes, Jenny, *darling!*" There was the merest hint of sarcasm in his tone.

With growing uneasiness Bree watched Jennifer's possessive attitude toward Neville. She held on to him, ordered him around, made him the butt of her little jokes and jibes to the crew.

Bree almost forgot her promise until she noticed Neville looking over the faces beyond the set, a frown making a crease in his makeup. Bree stepped around a couple of young men setting up a light, into his line of vision. He saw her and smiled, relaxing.

"All right! All right!" Martell charged around the camera car. "I want everybody who doesn't belong here off the set—now!"

Jennifer's attendants moved off with reluctance. Martell spied Brianne, a little too close to suit him.

"That means you—"

"She stays, Kurt," Neville rumbled ominously, startling him and Jennifer. "I want my escort close by at all times."

"Anything you say," Martell conceded with a shrug. "But, please, stand over here, okay?" he said to Bree, indicating a place near him.

Jennifer eyed the crowd suspiciously, unable to see beyond the lights glaring down on her, then looked back to Neville, cuddling closer to his arm—the hand of which remained adamantly in his jacket pocket.

"All right, everybody, places please!" the assistant director called.

"—and 'Digger,'" Martell said, turning to Neville again, "do you think you could take your hand out of your pocket for the shot, please?"

Chapter Ten

Neville relaxed more and more as the work progressed. But alarm at his reaction to Jennifer had taken root in Bree's mind. She found herself mentally pulling at it. The key to her uneasiness was some annoying recent occurrence buried in her memory, trying to resurface.

After each take and during filming breaks, Neville came over to her. After that first uncertain encounter with Jennifer, he'd loosened up, his self-assurance restored. The more the model fawned over him, the more distant he became, laughing and joking with the crew, complaining with them about delays, earning their affection.

Feeling more like an outsider than ever, Bree looked at her watch. Except for a short break for lunch, furnished compliments of the club, they'd been at it for seven hours. She had to leave soon to pick up Neville's tux before the store closed.

"This looks like it's going to go on for some time yet, Nanny," Neville muttered. "Why don't you go home? I'm over my jitters now, and I'll have Mickey drop me off home tonight. It was my fault you got home late last night—and up again so early this morning." He hugged her shoulders, his eyes running over her face with a look that drew an answering warmth from Bree's heart.

"I want you fresh and ready for tomorrow night." Then he added something that should have dispelled any fears she had about his strange behavior with Jennifer. "The kind of beauty you possess will forever outshine the Jennifer Thrales of this world."

He surprised her and everyone else, Jennifer included, by leaning down to kiss her long and hard.

"See you in the morning," he whispered and returned to the set.

Somehow she managed to find her way through the maze of trucks, grips, gaffers, and silks without tripping over any of them on her way to the car where she sat for a long time before turning the key in the ignition.

Errant, disjointed thoughts chased through her mind. The one she most dreaded almost broke through.

You can't go on this way, she told herself.

In only two more days he'll be gone! herself argued back.

And then what?

When Bree got home, she found a breathless Karen waiting for her and anxious to hear all about her week with Neville Ross.

"I can't believe it! I leave town for a few days and you snare a football pro to keep you company!" Karen bubbled in wonder. She'd changed from her uniform into jeans and a faded old pink sweatshirt. Tousling her already disarranged tawny curls, she stuffed a pillow behind her head, propped her feet on the coffee table, and leaned back while nursing a glass of iced tea between breathless questions.

"Soccer, not football," Bree corrected.

"Neville Ross! I can't believe it!" Karen ignored her.

"Believe it! Believe it!" Bree said waving a hand. "If

you just got back, how did you find out about—"

"Jack called before you came in," she said. "My friend Fran had him on the L.A. to Chicago flight two weeks ago and all she's talked about since is Neville Ross. He's as great a guy as he looks, she said. So, ah— how are you two getting along, anyway?" She fixed Bree with a probing look.

"He is—very nice. Kind and thoughtful to everyone," she paused remembering his antics with Jennifer, "unimpressed with his own importance, and easy going—"

"You *like* him," Karen observed astutely.

"Don't make anything of it, matchmaker! I'm only his gofer for the week."

"I think it's more than that." She set her glass down on the table to cross her arms behind her head. "By the way, whatever happened to Mr. Wonderful? I noticed his picture is gone from the drawing board— thank goodness."

"You'll be happy to hear that we broke up."

"No, I'm not happy to hear it because I know how crazy you were about him, but I do believe it's for the best. You deserve better than that self-centered showboat, Bree."

They were silent for a minute.

"Besides," Karen threw in half-jokingly, "look what happened! No sooner did the Lord shoo Mr. Kenyon out of your life than He sent in Neville Ross. Now that's what I call an answer to prayer. Wish He'd answer some of mine that generously."

"*Karen!*" Bree objected, laughing, "I don't even know if Neville's a Christian. How can you say he's an answer to prayer? And I wasn't even asking! Besides, silly, he's only passing through here on his way to New York."

"You think what you like and I'll think what I like. By the way, how often have you been seeing each other?"

"Every day. I'm his driver."

"Marvelous!"

"It's just business, Karen."

Karen suddenly noticed the tux Bree held in its garment bag. "What's that? A new dress? How dare you go shopping without me!" she chided, jumping from the sofa to run over for a peek.

"Well..." she looked askance at Bree. "I know tuxes for women are in, but isn't this one a bit large for you?"

"It's not mine. It's Neville's. I told you I'm his gofer for the week." Bree twitched the bag away and hung it on the closet door hook.

"What's the occasion?"

"Black tie dinner for the unveiling of the new Manta. I have to go with him...."

Karen laughed in triumph.

"There! I knew it was more than just business. Don't tell me he asked you to go with him just because you're his driver. He *did* ask you?"

"Yes..."

"—when he could have asked any number of other women he's met during the week—"

"Karen," Bree interrupted, glad she hadn't mentioned their encounter with Jennifer Thrale. "I was handy. It was convenient. Now, I have a big day tomorrow—and I just don't feel like talking any more, okay?"

Karen gave her an astute look and sighed.

"Okay." She said it with a slow smile. "I won't tease you anymore about it."

Suddenly feeling very tired and unaccountably sad, Bree turned to go down the hall to her room.

"How come you haven't returned your application to C.S.C yet? Deadline's soon, you know," Karen's accusing voice follower her.

"I want to pray about it some more," Bree put her off wearily.

"There's a time for praying and a time for *doing*. By the way, don't forget to call Jack before you go to bed. He had some bug in his brain about talking to you when he called...."

The phone rang early, before Bree woke next morning.

She heard Karen—up early brewing coffee and tinkering around the house—pad to the kitchen from the living room to answer it in a whisper.

"Oh!" she exclaimed with a start. "Oh, yes! Just a minute—I'll get her."

Before the muffled rush of slippered footsteps had reached her door, Bree had a pretty good idea who was calling. She was already into her robe and out the door nearly running over Karen calling, "Bree! It's *him!*"

"Calm down!" she told her cousin.

"His *voice* is even gorgeous!" Karen squeaked, prancing with excitement.

"Hello," Bree panted into the phone, breathless from her sprint.

"I'll go, I'll go," Karen backed off at a look from Bree and returned to the living room. Bree knew she'd have another interrogation to go through after the call.

"Well, does that heavy breathing mean you missed me?"

"Such conceit!"

"I missed you," he said quietly. She didn't know if it was the flirtatious Neville trying for a reaction or the more serious one she'd seen Thursday night. All the ambiguities of their relationship resurfaced to haunt her anew. "Now, Ms. Tyler, what time may I look forward to seeing you at Castle Ross with my tux?"

"How about in an hour?" She could have kicked herself. An hour? How could she possibly be presentable and get there in an hour?

"Done! We're going to be pressed for time today;

the shooting yesterday didn't go well. We have some finishing up to do today, much to Mickey's dismay! So, the sooner the better. See you in an hour!" He rattled it off and hung up before she could ask for more time.

"Nuts!" she cried and raced to shower, dress, and have enough time in case she got lost in the wilds of Birmingham again.

At least the haste got her out of Karen's cross-examination, Bree mused, driving the route to the house by the lake. It was becoming more familiar. She only got lost once this time!

She pulled into the drive, took the tux in its bag from the hook in the back seat and went to the door. The smell of the cedars was made stronger by the heat of the sun, and she inhaled it gratefully.

It took a few minutes before he answered her knock. He was dressed in slacks and pastel plaid shirt when he finally did swing the big door open for her. She hoped she didn't present too disreputable a picture. She'd pulled her hair back in a pony tail and braided it, and just jumped into the handiest pair of jeans in her closet. A crocheted teal cotton sweater topped off her hastily chosen outfit. The scooped neck was a little more open than she would have chosen otherwise, but....

His eyes lighted with approval at the sight of her.

"Got you out of bed, did I?" he accused with a grin. "Come in and make yourself comfortable—I've got a call—"

There wasn't much of any place to go except the piano bench. He hadn't relieved her of the tux, and she didn't think it would be a good idea to crumple it by lounging on one of the pillows on the floor.

"Yes, Mrs. Naismith," Neville spoke into the phone, making a wry face at Bree, "I *know* you'd all be happy to see me...Yes, Mum would be pleased if I'd go, but I don't know if my schedule will allow it." He laughed helplessly at Bree and held the phone away from his ear for a moment.

Bree heard the chattering of a woman's voice going at a breathless pace. Neville shrugged and shook his head, smiling.

"Won't allow what?" Bree asked suspiciously.

He covered the mouthpiece with his hand.

"Mrs. Naismith is an old friend of Mum's from the church we used to attend here. She wants me to come to services tomorrow," he explained. "*Yes,* Mrs. Naismith! I'm listening!" he hastened to assure his caller, taking his hand away.

Bree grinned wickedly.

"Your schedule *will* allow it," she said loudly enough for Mrs. Naismith to hear her.

Neville winced at the exclamation of glee on the other end of the line.

"All right," he said facing her after the call. He frowned, crossing his arms, but his mouth twitched at the corners. "If it will please you, I'll go."

"It will please both of us," Bree said.

"Both?" he said quizzically.

"Mrs. Naismith and me!"

He laughed and came toward her, the expression in his eyes changing.

Bree felt suddenly afraid. Not of him, but of herself and her own emotions, what she might do here, alone with him, under the influence of that look.

"Do I get to see what I've been hauling around since last evening?" She shook the feeling and thrust the hanger out to him.

He held her gaze a minute longer, then took the hanger from her and held it dangling between them.

"No," he said in answer to her question and grinned teasingly. "It's a surprise, and you have to wait till tonight, just like I do."

"Spoilsport," she accused, rising from the bench to make her way to the door.

"What's the hurry?" Surprised, he trailed after her. "I thought we could have breakfast together before I go to this confounded filming—"

There was more than a trace of annoyance in his tone.

"What happened last night after I left?" she asked innocently. "Everything seemed to be going so well—" Remembering his kiss at her departure, she thought she probably already had the answer.

"Jenny darling blew her lines consistently, and everything had to be reshot. I tell you—" he strode away from her, eyes flashing angrily, "We all felt *she* should be shot! Mickey's budget was ruined, Kurt's schedule was ruined, and my dinner was ruined as well!"

He whirled at a choking noise behind him to face her.

"And just what do you find so amusing?" he frowned, but she was wise to this subterfuge now. The dimple in his left cheek trembled into sight with his effort to maintain a severe expression.

"Never mind," he stopped her. "You'll only say something impertinent."

"I've had a good teacher when it comes to impertinence," she pointed out and flinched.

Wrong thing to do, Tyler! she realized when she opened her eyes to find herself in his arms.

"Oh!" she gasped uncertainly.

"I really was looking forward to breakfast—with you, that is." he amended.

"But I thought you were in a hurry. You said on the phone—"

"To see *you*," he said.

Oh, Neville, please don't tease! It's not fun any more, she thought.

He held her back a little, distressed at what he saw in her face.

"Brianne, what's wrong?"

"Nothing. It's just—I can't go to breakfast with you

because I promised my brother I'd go to his son's scrimmage this morning—" She got no further.

"*Scrimmage?* What kind of scrimmage?" he demanded. "Not *soccer?*"

"Yes." She sighed.

"Ho!" he shouted and released her to make a dash for the hall, disappearing into one of the doorways.

"Let's go," he said, reappearing with a light khaki jacket tied around his shoulders.

"But what about the commercial?" she reminded him.

"I told Kurt I wouldn't be available till ten. Let Ms. Thrale wait for *me* for a change, eh?" With a wicked laugh he shooed her through the door.

Since the east side was Bree's home territory, Neville let her drive. They found the field in St. Clair Shores and made their way down the sidelines through a gaggle of parents, looking for her brother. Bree recognized him by his "lucky" red baseball jacket and led Neville in his direction.

Jack stood absorbed, watching the scrambling mass of small bodies at one end of the field, a clipboard in one hand. He periodically thrust the other through his dark hair in excitement or exasperation. Two small boys shadowed his agitated pacing up and down the side of the field.

Neville, intent on the progress of the two tiny teams, bumped into Bree when she stopped behind her brother.

"Sorry," he mumbled in apology, catching Jack's attention.

"Bree!" Jack caught her in an enthusiastic hug.

"I made it, as you can see!" she returned his noisy kiss.

"Is this—?" his eyes slid to Neville standing behind her.

"Jack, this is my *nursling,*" she emphasized the

133

word for Neville's benefit, "Neville Ross—ex-soccer pro cum author, cum actor—"

"Come off it!" To Jack's amusement Neville gave her a squeeze as he moved her aside to shake hands with Jack. "Pleased, Tyler."

"Wow." Normally effusive, Jack mumbled as he shook Neville's hand.

"I never realized *you* were a soccer fan, Jack," Bree mused.

"So you're one of the brothers this woman routinely terrorized," Neville said.

Jack's laughter crackled. "Yeah! Did she tell you about the time she chased me with a broom and—"

"No! *Do* go on!" Neville encouraged with great interest, but a ball rolled off the field and came to a stop at his feet. He leaned over to pick it up, relinquishing it to the player who had the "throw-in."

"Which one is yours?" He turned again to Jack.

"The little brunet with the baggy socks," Jack pointed out, ruefully smiling with paternal pride.

"You're coaching as well, I see." Neville looked with curiosity at the scribbled diagrams on the clipboard.

"Yeah," Jack admitted with a nervous laugh. "It's a first for *all* of us."

"Coach Jack, when can *I* go in?" a small querulous voice at Jack's side broke in.

"In a minute, Jason, at the next substitution."

Bree watched Neville look down at Jason, coppery hair shining in the sun. His gold and blue jersey hung out of oversized blue shorts, socks, and shin guards seemingly too big for the spindly little legs.

A secret smile curved Neville's lips when he looked up again.

"It's a great game, Jason," he said distractedly to the boy.

"Yeah, I know!" Jason fired back petulantly. "*I* wanna go out and play too!"

"Okay, Jas, okay!" Jack told him, "Hold your horses, will ya?"

They watched a while longer, Jack glancing over to Neville uneasily whenever he made a move.

"You're doing fine!" Neville hastened to assure him when he realized what the problem was. He reached around Bree to clap Jack on the back. "I only hope I do as well when it's my turn to coach in the 'munchkin' league!"

"Oh yeah?" Jack was suddenly all interest, but the referee's whistle reminded him of unfinished business. "Ref! Sub!" he yelled, sending Jason charging onto the field to replace another player.

Immediately another small voice piped up.

"Coach Jack, when can *I* go in?"

Bree and Neville laughed. Jack shook his head, promising to send the boy in as soon as he could.

"But what's that you say—" Jack tenaciously returned to the subject Neville broached before the interruption. "—you're thinking of coaching an 'under eight' team? When?"

"Oh, not for a while yet!" Neville stopped him with a laugh. "But one of these days I hope to coach my own son—"

Bree felt uncomfortable with the direction of the conversation between two of the most notorious teases she'd ever known.

"*You* have a son?" Jack asked quickly. He threw a bewildered look at Bree.

"No. Not yet, that is," Neville corrected, chuckling, "but someday hopefully." He spoke to Jack but gave Bree a long look that wasn't lost on her incorrigible brother. She knew she'd hear about it later.

What are you trying to tell me? she questioned the look. *Why don't you just say something if—*

He threw an arm around Bree and gave her a hug. It could have meant anything from easy-going camaraderie to just plain delight at watching his favorite game played by a bunch of budding 'Digger' Rosses.

"Head it! *Head* it!" he yelled excitedly to an under-sized defender, caught up in the spirit of the practice game. "You know, they didn't have this league when I was their age. Soccer was practically unknown in the States. I think it's just fantastic they're learning it so young now."

After a foray downfield, Jack returned to the former direction of Neville's conversation.

"Does that mean you're planning to settle down soon then? No more life in the fast lane?" he asked laughing, and nudged Bree.

Bree wanted to strangle him.

Neville smiled over her head, still hugging her to his side.

"Probably, Tyler," he said with a wink at Jack that Bree missed. "I'm closer to packing it all away than I've ever been."

Chapter Eleven

"I wish I'd had a broom!" Bree fumed, charging around the apartment in her robe that evening. "I'd give Jack a taste of the old days for setting me up that way—give *both* of them a taste of the broom! I was so embarrassed!"

"It's no use upsetting yourself," Karen soothed between choked guffaws. "I know what you mean about Jack. *Now* what are you looking for?"

Bree was on her hands and knees peering under the sofa's dust ruffle.

"I *know* I set those shoes out here before I took my shower—and now I can only find one of them. Look at the time!" she moaned jumping up to limp back to the bathroom in one high-heeled black satin sandal. "Just look at my *hair!*"

"Calm down," Karen ordered, taking the brush from her hands and pushing her down on the side of the tub. "Now just tell me how you want the rest of it...."

Bree fidgeted under Karen's deft hands as she arranged the dark glossy mass of hair into a sophisticated upsweep with a knot of curls at the crown.

"You look *gorgeous!*" Karen assured, leaning down, putting her face next to Bree's to get the effect in the mirror. "If he isn't in love with you yet, he will be—" she started irrepressibly.

"Karen, *please!*" Bree wailed, cutting her off. "I have enough on my mind without worrying about lovesick jocks...."

It was a lame joke. It wasn't the lovesick jock she was worried about but the jock's lovesick escort.

No-o-o, Tyler! Don't even think it! she cringed trying to calm her nerves. *He's only business! This evening is only business!*

The trick was losing its effectiveness.

"Here," Karen was holding the red silk dress down for her to step into. "Now be careful and don't catch your heel in the hem. What time did you say you have to pick him up?" Karen adjusted the spaghetti-thin straps on her shoulders.

"I'm not. He said he's picking *me* up. How he wangled a car—"

"*Here?*" It was Karen's turn to panic. "*He's* coming *here?*"

"Karen! Come back here and finish zipping me!" Puzzled, Bree followed her cousin's fleeing form. "What are you doing, you crazy person?"

Karen had dragged the vacuum from the closet and plugged it in, frantically pushing it back and forth over the living room carpet.

"Here's your other shoe." She picked up the web of thin straps and heel from under the chair, tossing it to Bree.

"Karen, Karen!" Bree giggled helplessly at the sight. "It's all right. The place looks fine," she tried to assure the flying figure. "Besides, he'll be here any minute."

On cue there was a polite, determined rapping on the door.

They looked at each other, then flew in opposite directions: Bree back to the bedroom and Karen and the vacuum to the closet.

Bree heard her cousin's feet patter back down the hall and slow to a dignified pace as she approached the door.

138

"Hello—" Karen's perky voice stopped in midgreeting.

In her mind's eye, Bree could see the awed expression on Karen's face as she dreamwalked backward to let Neville Ross in.

"Good evening!" Neville's voice replied, pleasantly surprised. "I expected you to look different, Brianne, but not totally *transformed!*"

"Oh! but I'm not—that is—" Bree heard Karen's confused stutter. "Bree's—"

"—not quite ready yet. I expected that." The rumble of his deep-voiced laughter drifted down the hall. "I'm Neville Ross, by the way. Who might you be?"

"Ah—I'm cousin's Bree—Bree's cousin!" Karen corrected herself.

"And do you have a name, cousin?" He was enjoying Karen's confusion while he tried to put her at her ease.

The murmur of voices moved out of range while Bree finished her makeup. A touch more mascara to emphasize the eyes; the moss green shadow to bring out the green of her changeable eyes, no need for pencil—luckily, her brows arched darkly and naturally enough without it.

Hands shaking nervously she poked black onyx ball earrings into her earlobes, fixed the backs, and took a last swipe at her lips with the gloss before turning to the door.

Karen popped in, eyes wide and staring.

"He's everything Fran said he was!" she croaked and collapsed on the bed with laughter. "I made *such* a fool of myself!"

"With his aiding and abetting every step of the way," Bree suspected. "He's a worse tease than Jack, if you can imagine such a thing."

Karen sat up.

"You look *ter-r-r-ific*, cuz!" she said giving Bree an acute once-over.

"Are you *sure?*" Terror seized Bree. She gave her image one last check in the full-length mirror on the closet door. The simple styling of the red Chinese silk made it elegant. The top draped gracefully, caught at the waist by a braided black silk belt, and curved from where it crossed in front to make a slit revealing her slender ankles when she walked.

"I'm positive. He'll adore you—if he doesn't already," Karen added mischievously. Exasperated, Bree turned to go.

"Here! Don't forget these!" Karen jumped up to thrust Bree's black beaded bag and silk evening wrap in her hands.

Neville had his back to her when she entered the living room. He was studying the contents of her open sketchbook on the drawing board.

She took a deep breath. The whisper of silk as she moved caught his attention. He spun around and stopped.

For a long moment they stood studying one another.

"Well," he said softly, taking a step toward her. "Well."

His eyes traveled her length to take in the red gown and returned to rest on her face. A shadow flitted behind his eyes, but he said lightly, "Words fail me."

"*That* must be a first," Bree countered immediately.

He laughed and the mood was broken. Bree saw with surprise that with his regulation black tuxedo he wore a red satin tie and cummerbund.

"So *that's* why you wanted to know what color I was wearing."

"We're a matched set—" he said coming over to her. He held a piece of paper in his hand that looked vaguely familiar. "I've been looking through your work—" He waved a hand at the drawing board. "Brianne, it's very *good!* You have an enviable talent. With a little training it could be formidable. Why haven't you returned this to the registrar?"

The paper he held out to her was the half-finished application for the graphic arts academy.

"I wasn't sure about it," she hedged. Drawing a deep breath she voiced her reservations. "I wasn't sure it was the direction the Lord wanted me to pursue...."

"Are you sure it was the Lord and not a distraction in the form of a certain Mr. *Kenyon?*"

She heard Karen, lounging against the door behind her, snicker at that.

She and Neville locked glances. He wasn't teasing now.

For a minute she felt they were all ranged against her: Neville, Karen, and Jack.

"I see you two have been discussing me—"

"One only discusses persons one cares about," he pointed out coolly. "And from what Karen says it's the general consensus of all of us who care about you that you see to this as soon as possible. You owe it to yourself—yes, and to your Lord, too. It doesn't make sense for Him to give you an ability he didn't intend for you to use." He called to Karen. "Isn't that right?"

"Absolutely!"

Bree was outgunned.

"Now—I've been thinking—I have a friend in graphic arts," he plunged ahead not giving her a chance to interrupt. "I'm going to speak to him about taking you on when this assignment ends Monday so you can work at your craft while you learn it."

She stared at him in disbelief. He'd charged in here tonight to take her to a party and had ended up resolving her career dilemma in one short imperative speech.

"Does that meet with your approval?" he cocked an eyebrow in question at her.

It was no coincidence. When this many people voiced the same opinion, she knew it was one of the ways the Lord used to guide her.

141

One down, one to go, she thought, looking at Neville.

"Yes—Nanny!" she nodded. Neville laughed, obviously relieved. Perhaps he'd expected a debate.

"You two better get moving," Karen reminded them.

"Right!" Neville agreed, helping Bree into the wisp of silk, dolman-sleeved jacket. "You're trembling!"

"I'm *nervous,*" she moaned. "I've never been to anything this formal before."

"Nothing to it." He snapped his fingers. "Stick with me...."

"And I'll go places, right?"

He bustled her out the door with a laugh.

"I'll be thinking of you," Karen assured, chuckling after them.

"Thanks!" Bree called back over her shoulder. "I need someone to think of me!"

Still laughing softly, Karen closed the door and leaned against it. "The way those two looked at each other," she mused, "they *both* do."

Brianne was still apprehensive when they entered the drive of McBain's home. Neville had somehow managed to borrow or lease a red Mercedes roadster for the evening, and only her threat of violent retribution kept him from putting down the top on the drive from her apartment.

"On the way home," she told him. "Then it won't matter how my hair looks."

"Well!" he took affront. "So you don't care how it looks for *me*—is that it?"

"No," she pouted at him. "But if you lower the top without giving me a scarf to cover my hair you deserve to look at the results."

"Blast!" he muttered, peering through the windshield. "The place is parked solid. We'll have a bit of a walk—although that *can* have its advantages," he grinned.

"Please behave." She gave him a pleading look.

"You're making a big fuss over nothing," he tried to reassure her, guiding her to the house after they'd parked. "You have a great deal of presence and poise—and you look smashing."

He leaned over to nibble the tip of her ear before she knew what he intended, then assisted her up the piazza's stone steps. "After all, P.R. chose you as my escort. They obviously think you're up to snuff."

Parker led them in. Neville relinquished Bree's wrap to him and took Bree through the house to the terrace. There, among a dazzling, excited throng, Bree was quickly introduced by McBain to Jennifer Thrale among others, while Neville looked on noncommittally. Jennifer, outdazzling everyone in gold lamé, chatted animatedly with everyone around her, keeping a wary eye on Neville and pointedly ignoring Bree.

Bree was relieved when dinner was finally announced at eight, and they shifted to the airy dining room. Bree had never seen such a room before. The table was an immense expanse of white linen, sparkling china and crystal, and heavy sterling silver. There were at least thirty places set at the table.

"You'll do fine!" Neville whispered reassuringly in her ear as she hesitated at the dining room's glass doors.

Bree hoped her presence and poise lived up to his expectations and that she wouldn't stare too hard at the prismed crystal chandelier above the long table or swallow too loudly when she had to decide which of the four glasses at her place to drink from first.

"The water's always a safe bet," Neville instructed, taking a sip from the large, faceted goblet before his plate.

She looked her thanks.

Jennifer, she noted gratefully, was seated down the

table at McBain's right while she and Neville were at Eleanor's right on the opposite end.

The long dinner with its many courses passed without mishap under Neville's guidance. He brought her through with confidence. She even relaxed enough to enjoy the lively conversation going on around them, much of it instigated or abetted by Neville himself. Just being with him made it enjoyable.

Eleanor's eyes rested on them frequently. Bree noticed and wondered what she must be thinking about her presence as Neville's date. But aside from an occasional knowing smile, she was graciously accepting.

McBain beamed at her unreservedly, a response not lost to Jennifer's sharp observation.

After what seemed an interminable time, the meal ended. McBain, announcing that press and photographers were getting restless for the unveiling, invited everyone to the fountain court for the big event.

"Neville, *darling!*" Jennifer sidled up between him and Brianne and possessed herself of his arm. "You've been ignoring me all evening!"

Brianne stood back politely but noted with a thrill of hope the look of exasperation that crossed Neville's face.

"*Jenny,* darling," he mimicked subtly. He was still a little uneasy in her presence, maintaining a polite reserve, a hint of something unspoken but assumed between them. "Shall we go do our little song and dance for the media?"

Puzzled, Bree looked after them. Neville shot her a speculative glance over his shoulder as they moved off, Jennifer trying to monopolize his attention. He looked worried—about what? Bree's reaction, or his own?

Watching them from the back of the crowd as the official unveiling went on, Bree was more puzzled than ever by the tension between the attractive couple. Plagued by the feeling that the piece of infor-

144

mation that would unlock the puzzle of their interaction was locked in her mind somewhere, she wandered away. On the terrace, Parker refilled her fluted glass with water.

"…it was all her fault too," two voices at the edge of the crowd, their owners hidden by the carefully cultivated topiary, broke into her thoughts. With a start she recognized the speaker as Gena. "But all her hanging around won't do her any good!"

"Yes," a second voice replied cattily, "It was a clever trick, getting herself assigned to him as an escort, but in the end he'll go back to Jennifer—just like he always does. Just yesterday she said in an interview they've set the date for—"

Bree burned with shock and humiliation. Her stomach gave a sickening lurch as an unnamed hope died. She backed into the shadow of the tall shrubbery to try to compose herself.

But that was the missing piece; everything fit together now. The broken picture frame Tuesday, his sudden withdrawal Wednesday night when she'd mentioned Jennifer, the coolness to the model the past couple of days. In the back of her mind, she'd *known* he was engaged to her and had been for some time. Their appearances at dazzling functions were detailed frequently in the paper's celebrity columns.

Stupid! she accused herself. *Jack knew! Karen knew too! Why didn't you know? Just didn't want to remember? Stupid! Stupid! Stupid! Why didn't you see?*

She took deep breaths to hold back the building storm of emotion, but her conscience continued to tear into her. She'd been tripped up in her own clever game. All his attentions, all the flattery had been his way of getting back at Jennifer. He was using her just as she'd planned to use him.

She stifled a sob with the back of her hand.

"Brianne! Is that you?" Neville's voice called as swift footsteps approached her hiding place. She had to pull herself together quickly! This was *one* time she refused to be honest with him when he demanded to know the cause of her distress! He hadn't been honest with *her!*

"What are you doing here—" He pulled the branches aside and drew her back onto the path. "You're pale as a sheet! Brianne—"

"I was feeling a little ill," she said brushing aside his concern with a shaky laugh. "All that apprehension went right to my stomach."

He examined her face closely, tipping it back into the light.

"You are looking a bit peaked," he murmured. His brows drew down in a frown. "I'll go get the car and make our excuses to Nell and Mickey."

She pulled her chin out of his hand.

"No!" she objected. "That isn't necessary. I can go sit for a while in the powder room."

"I won't hear of it," he dismissed the suggestion, puzzled by her behavior. "What are you trying to hide from me now, Brianne?"

He put a hand up to touch her face and she turned it away. He grabbed her roughly by both arms and made her face him again. "Now that's enough of that!" he commanded. "What's happened since I left you—did someone say something out of line—"

"No!" she evaded. "I—just remembered something—"

"What?" he demanded suspiciously

"My *place!* That's what!' she replied. "I just suddenly felt ashamed of the way I've been carrying on with you, as if you weren't—"

"Weren't *what!*" he asked dangerously when she paused.

"Engaged!" she said. She drew a deep breath as she faced him.

"*That* says it all!" He threw up his hands, frustrated, taking a couple of steps from her. "And you think I've been leading you on, is that it?"

"Something like that."

"Brianne," his voice sad, he spoke again, "do you *truly* think I'm such a heel as that?"

She looked away, embarrassed. She realized she knew him well enough to eliminate that possibility.

"No," she gave him grudgingly.

"Thank you." He paced meditatively, turned, and came back. "I hadn't planned to mention it yet, but yes—I *was*—now pay close attention to that little word *was!*" he emphasized. "I *was* engaged to Jenny-darling for a long time! I am no longer. Advanced age does bring with it a certain amount of wisdom," he explained with a melancholy smile. "We were both fortunate to get out of it before it turned into a marriage."

"*There* you are." Eleanor McBain appeared from the direction of the fountain court. "I've been looking for you to provide a little musical relief for us, my dear." She laughed at Neville, the pearl-gray chiffon of her gown shimmering in the wan moonlight. She stopped abruptly, looking from one to the other of them. "Am I interrupting something?"

"No," Neville assured her quickly, "Brianne was feeling a bit punk. We just stepped out for a little air."

"Well, there's certainly very little of it stirring out here!" Nell observed with a smile, going over to Brianne. "My dear, would you like to lie down a while? The upstairs powder room will probably be a lot cooler." She patted Bree's shoulder in concern.

"No, thank you so much, but I'm fine now!" Bree said quickly.

"Besides, Nell, if you insist on tormenting your other guests with my out-of-practice playing, I'll need Brianne around for moral support," Neville said. He slipped a hand under her arm and pulled her gently along with him after Nell as they started back to the house.

There was no chance to continue the discussion.

147

When they entered the air-conditioned music room through French doors overlooking the terrace, Jennifer, who'd been watching for Neville, attached herself to his side again.

"Oh, darling, do play that favorite of mine from *All's Fair!* You know how I love it—you used to play it for me all the time!" she finished with an arch look at Bree. The diamond-shaped facets of her metallic gown flashed with every move, putting Bree in mind of a Christmas tree wreathed with twinkle lights.

"No, I think I'm in more of a Bach mood at the moment," Neville said. He peeled her fingers off his bicep with a polite smile and seated himself at the piano.

"Here, dear, sit by me," Nell invited Bree. She'd drawn up a couple of the exquisite Sheraton chairs that sat around the pastel-blue-and-white music room. Bree was sure they were the *real* thing, and not reproductions.

"No, I'd like her to stand there." Neville indicated the door post directly in his line of vision at the end of the long piano. "Moral support, you know!" he winked at Nell.

Bree left Nell reluctantly. At least several of the other guests stood also, still in their conversational groups, so she didn't feel too obvious.

Neville wiggled his eyebrows up and down at her, then slipped into Bach's "Prelude in C." His playing was far from out of practice. He sailed through the piece with ease, glancing up frequently to watch her expression.

At its conclusion, a sigh of appreciation went up with the polite applause. Jennifer, who'd stationed herself at his left side, sauntered around to his right and lounged in the curve of the piano's case. To her annoyance, however, no matter how she tried to obstruct his view of Brianne, he shifted just enough on the bench to see around her.

His long fingers roamed over the keys playing bits of

other pieces and disjointed melodies.

"*Now* play my song," Jennifer demanded, sulking. Bree saw his mouth tighten, and he launched into a very rapid, expressionless rendition of the popular song. Jennifer glanced over her shoulder with a smug expression at Bree, but her eyes were on Neville.

At its conclusion he continued immediately into a Beethoven selection. She smiled, recognizing it as the theme of a classical music radio program in Detroit, one she'd said was her favorite, a movement from the "Pathetique" sonata. He returned her smile slowly and held her eyes with his.

She started to look away under the intent gaze, but he lifted his eyebrows in a gesture asking her to keep her eyes on him. She saw just for a moment the expression that had been in his eyes Thursday night before he'd kissed her. Only now it seemed to be asking for *her* understanding and support. He was having a hard time dealing with Jennifer, despite the fact their relationship was over. Bree smiled. She *did* understand that. She settled back against the doorjamb, and confident in her silent encouragement, he returned the smile and his attention to the keyboard.

Jennifer, Mike Kozara, and several others of the old friends he'd threatened her with Wednesday closed around him with enthusiastic compliments when he finished playing. Bree slipped out on the terrace to think and wandered to the spot she'd hidden in earlier.

Her thoughts were in turmoil. Tomorrow was Neville's last day in town. He wouldn't be needing her officially after tonight till she took him back to Metro tomorrow afternoon. Briefly she thought of his invitation for Sunday brunch with the McBains. He'd never pursued the subject. Had he forgotten?

She heard the crunch of shell paving under foot, and before she could turn to see who it was, Neville's arms slipped around her.

"Are you all right?" he asked solicitously, nuzzling

her neck. She drew an involuntary breath at the contact, feeling as if she could melt backward into his substantial form.

"Fine," she said.

"That was for you, you know," he chuckled into her ear, "you and Karl!" His arms tightened around her.

"Still fond of cavorting with the help, I see." Jennifer, a golden glow in the dimness of the garden, sauntered around to confront them, contempt for Bree in her eyes.

Bree tried unobtrusively to pull away from Neville's embrace, but it only tightened more, his fingers wrapping around her upper arms almost uncomfortably.

"Jennifer, I believe you've met Brianne, my good friend and invaluable aid this past week." Neville fielded Jennifer's insult smoothly and without rancor.

"I rather suspected you had someone tucked away by the way you've avoided me the past few days." Jennifer faced them, her eyes sliding warily from one to the other. Long gleaming nails combed the metallic tassel at the end of her corded tie belt. "But if you're quite over your little 'mad' now don't you think it would be kinder and in Miss Tyler's best interests to dismiss her, before she becomes any more attached to you?"

"Jennifer!" Neville growled in warning.

"Really, Neville, we have a great many things to discuss yet!" she continued, her voice rising.

Bree supposed she probably had a lot more at stake than Neville realized, having given the press information he was about to refute

"—there were a great many annoying little details to finalize in our plans—"

"We *have* no plans, Jen," Neville said emphatically. Bree heard the hard edge in his voice. "*You* made that *very* clear last month. The past is over, Jen, and I no longer have any interest or desire to call it back!"

Bree squirmed in his hold. She felt like an eavesdropper on a replay of her confrontation with Spence.

"You mean you're really seriously doing this!"

Bree realized her presence was goading Jennifer into a jealous frenzy as much as Neville's implacable stance.

"—throwing me over for an office junior!" She gave an ugly laugh of disbelief.

Bree almost laughed herself, despite the attempt at insult.

But Neville responded quickly. "You know, Jen, your refusal to accept truth always annoyed me more than any of your other peccadilloes."

"Well, if we're going to fling peccadilloes—" Jennifer countered, apparently more than willing to do so.

"Stop it!" Bree struggled in Neville's grasp. "If you're going to argue, at least let me leave!"

He held her fast.

"No—I won't let you go. And I am not about to embark on another long and pointless discussion with Jennifer!" he said.

Jennifer stiffened with defiance as he looked her coldly in the eyes from over Brianne's shoulder.

"We said everything that needed saying five weeks ago. So, good night, Jennifer, darling." Jennifer took a step toward him as if to respond, but he said again, with finality, "*Good night,* Jennifer!"

She flung the shredded tassel down and stalked off a few feet, then turned back at the terrace step for a parting shot.

"*Don't* think you can come crawling back in another month, when your fascination with your new toy wears off, Neville Ross! This is the absolute end of my patience with you!"

"I wish you had let me go," Bree muttered miserably.

"What—and let you miss a perfectly splendid fight? I should think not!"

"You just used me to get back at her!"

"And didn't you do the same?"

She went cold at the warning in his voice.

"What do you mean?" she asked, but she knew.

"Kenyon!" he replied with distaste. "Wasn't all your attention to me just to get back at him?"

After a long silence she admitted, "Yes."

"Thank you for your honesty. It's one of the things I've most admired about you," he whispered kissing her ear. "I saw what it was yesterday, just before the match."

"Is *that* why you trampled him so!" she marveled. A short laugh escaped her as she remembered Spence's reaction to Neville after the game.

"I'm not normally such a clod," he explained, but she could hear the smile in his voice. "I must say, I did rather enjoy it."

"But—how did you *know?*"

"I saw it in your eyes the other night, at the house. When you've been through a broken relationship, sometimes you can see the symptoms in someone else," he said, tracing a path down her neck with his lips. "Besides, I eavesdropped when he gave you that dressing down yesterday."

She was sorting out the pieces. "Why did you break up with Jennifer? It's every man's dream to have someone like her—she's the perfect woman—beautiful, famous, successful in her work—"

"—And that's the rub," he interrupted, the hard edge coming back into his voice. "Her work was more important to her than I was. She refused to leave London and relocate in the States with me. We had quite a brannigan about it. But I guess we'd been growing apart for a long time, and I didn't realize it." He turned her by the shoulders to face him. "It's hard to break a habit sometimes, even when it's no longer fun."

"She must have been more than a habit at one time," Bree reproached. "I mean, you must have *loved* her, or you wouldn't have wanted to marry her."

All the reasons for a change of subject flooded to

her mind as he took her in his arms again, his lips hovering just above hers.

"And didn't you ever think you were in love with someone when it turned out not to be that at all?" It was a not-so-subtle reminder of her own recent lapse in romantic judgment. "Anyway, the rationale for that escapes me...."

He kissed her, but this time it was different—for both of them. She moved unreservedly into his embrace. It wasn't comfort or compassion on his part either. It had gone beyond that. He *did* care for her.

And she? There was no denying or hiding from it anymore. She was in love with him.

"Neville! Is that you out there?" McBain's voice pierced the night air. He stood silhouetted in the door of the music room trying to peer into the deep shadows beyond the terrace.

Brianne came to herself first, pulling out of his embrace, but he held her arms to keep her from slipping away.

"Second Corinthians again?" he questioned.

"What?" she asked, trying to compose herself before McBain came out looking for them.

"I'm here, Mickey," Neville called to him. "Give us a couple of minutes and we'll be right with you."

"Aha!" She heard McBain chuckle. "Sure thing, son. Don't take too long. Some of the guests are leaving and want to say good-bye."

"Now, about tomorrow," Neville returned to Brianne as McBain stepped back inside.

"Tomorrow is Sunday," she reminded him, surprised at how calm she sounded. "You have brunch with the McBains. Then you have to be at Metro at five."

She was reminding them both it was ending, over just as it was beginning. She felt limp and lifeless in his hands and wondered what he was feeling.

"I—ah—have a slight change," he said with a crooked smile. Whatever he felt, he kept it to himself.

153

"Mickey may not like it, but I'd rather go to church in the morning instead. Seems you've rather committed me to an appearance to appease Mrs. Naismith—*and* my mum. If she hears I *didn't* go I'll catch the very devil when she sees me again."

The image of this hulking man cowering before his mother caught her off guard and surprised a laugh from her. She forgot for a minute to wonder why the lightness of his attitude failed to match the depth of his response to her a few minutes earlier.

"Will you go with me?" he asked. His mood changed again. He was serious.

She thought about it. It would be disastrous now that she knew she loved him. Spending more time with him would only make tomorrow's farewell that much harder, would nurture an impossible hope.

"I don't think anyone will miss me too much at my church," she heard her turncoat mouth say, capitulating to the desire to be with him in spite of everything.

"Good! I'll pick you up at nine. Then we can make a day of it with lunch by the lake. You can help me pack and close up the house before we go to the airport." He planned their last day glibly.

Brianne felt hurt that he seemed to take it so lightly. Had she been mistaken about the commitment in his kiss? But did that really matter in light of the fact that, as far as she knew, he wasn't a Christian? Her promise loomed before her. But as always, when she remembered to trust, peace of mind returned. She *would* keep her promise, no matter what. Only God knew what might happen tomorrow—and maybe Neville wouldn't really leave after all.

"Let's go get this over with so I can get you home," he said, and he took her back to the party.

Chapter Twelve

Brianne was in an agony of uncertainty the next morning as she hurried to be ready when Neville arrived. She was grateful for Karen's restraint in not questioning her too closely about the dinner party the night before. She was also thankful Karen stopped teasing her about Neville. Perhaps it was because her feelings were so obvious, teasing was redundant?

Bree looked at her image in the bathroom mirror. She dropped her eyes. Yes, it was all *too* obvious. She turned away to avoid seeing the dazed, distant look of love in her eyes.

"What time did you say Neville's picking you up?" Karen's voice broke into her reverie. She'd stationed herself at the bay window to watch for him, confident this time that her home was ready for inspection. Bree suspected she'd spent all evening tearing it apart and putting it back together in a cleaning frenzy.

"He said nine," Bree told her absently. She fastened a single string of pearls around her neck and put in the matching earring studs. She put the finishing touches on her hair, sectioning it to sweep the upper part into a pearl-studded gold clasp at the top of her head, pulling it back to flow in soft waves around her shoulders. If the church they were attending didn't have air conditioning she knew she was in for a warm time of it. But he'd said he liked her hair down.

Come on, Tyler!

"Well, if he said nine, he either can't tell time or changed his mind. No one else in this place has a Mercedes like that. Come to think of it, no one else in this place has a Mercedes," Karen called from the living room.

"He *would* be early," Bree muttered, finishing her makeup and giving her wrists a quick touch of perfume. "Now where did I lay that jacket?"

"He's here!" Karen chirped, going to the door.

Bree made a dash for the bedroom and fussed around the closet for the white linen bolero jacket she'd planned to wear with her yellow sundress.

"Must have left it in the hall closet," she decided and wheeled out of her room to collide with Neville as he entered the door of the apartment.

"My apologies!" he laughed, catching her.

The look in his eyes as they met hers left her breathless.

They moved apart self-consciously under Karen's fascinated scrutiny.

"My apologies for being early also," he continued. "But I wasn't sure how long it would take to get to the church from this side of town....I hope it doesn't inconvenience you."

The last comment was to Karen who shrugged and rolled her eyes.

"Oh, no! Not at all! Can I get you some coffee or toast or something while Bree finishes getting dressed?" Knowing her house was in order made Karen more affable.

"No, thanks, I've already had as much as I need to shock me back to life this morning!" he laughed again.

"Besides, I'm already ready." Bree made a face at Karen, then smiled when her cousin tossed a crumpled paper napkin at her in return.

"You have a lovely place," Neville noted offhandedly to Karen. "I meant to say something last night—very homey and inviting." He looked approvingly around the room at the warm glow of polished wood and brass.

"Next time you're in town you'll have to come over for dinner—" Karen invited. "I'll even *cook* instead of sending out for pizza."

Bree smiled to see the old "Digger" Ross charm at work, but she knew he'd meant what he said.

"I'd love to," he accepted the offer.

"You're leaving this afternoon, Bree says." Karen walked to the door with them. She held out her hand and he shook it warmly. "Have a good flight and—" she caught herself with a giggle "—there I go sounding like a flight attendant!"

If he hadn't won her approval already by his comments about the apartment, he certainly did when he brushed a kiss across her cheek and said behind Bree, "I hope we do meet again soon, under happier circumstances."

"*Happier* circumstances?" Bree turned questioning eyes on him.

"Well, you can't say that having to leave before I've had a chance to spend much time in the company of two such lovely women..." he started to say.

"Really!" Bree cut him off.

"Oh no! Go on—go on!" Karen encouraged. She laughed to Bree, "You're right! He *is* worse than Jack!"

"Come along," Neville steered Bree out the door, "I'd like to make this a nice, leisurely drive so I can point out scenes of my childhood as we go...." and they left Karen for the second time shaking her head in wonder after them.

Bree's game with him was over. As they headed east out the Ford Freeway to the two exchanges that would eventually lead to the Bloomfield Hills church, she ruminated on the unexpected turn her plans had taken.

Not only had he put an end to her trifling with him,

but he'd reversed the order she'd been so intent on establishing Monday. *He'd* taken charge of the situation, and *he* was in control.

Their first stop in his private odyssey was the opposite side of the lake from his borrowed house.

"You can't see it from here," he said, handing her out of the car, "but that end of the lake where it narrows to go under the bridge gets quite shallow about this time of year. Sometimes I could cross it through the mud. A couple of other guys in the neighborhood and I would come over here and catch frogs and those big snails that used to be in the lake."

"I'm sure your mother just loved that," Bree grimaced.

This side of the lake was less meticulously manicured than the other. Underbrush tangled through the thicket of tall trees on the lake side of the residential street, in contrast to the carefully tended lots facing it.

"Oh, yes indeed," Neville agreed. "She would have loved it even more had we ever succeeded in capturing one of those fat Canadian geese over there. *That* was the height of our hunting ambitions."

The next stop wasn't really a stop. They drove slowly through the wooded hills to the church parking lot and sat in the car.

"No, let's not go in yet," he said as she collected her Bible and purse from the back seat. "I just want to sit here for a while first. In a way, this is a special place for me too, and I'd like to enjoy it in private with you."

He took her left hand with a smile and turned his gaze back to the scene before them. The parking lot was enclosed by a low stone wall of the same mellow gray granite as the church across the drive behind them. Ahead, in a depression between two grassy knolls, was a small pond, landscaped and with a low stone bench nearby.

She'd gotten a good look at Kirkwood Church when they pulled off the main road. Situated halfway up the low hill it looked like it had been picked up bodily from another century in the British Isles and dropped into the present, which turned out to be very near the truth.

"It was disassembled and shipped over from the old country, then reassembled just as it stood there. Of course, it's been modernized somewhat and renovated on the interior." Neville pointed out with a chuckle, "The members might like the old, but they're not ready to forego the comforts of the new, either!" There was proprietary pride in his attitude as he spoke, a softening of his expression as he regarded the church of his childhood.

Bright green shrubs dotted the walls of the church, providing a pleasant contrast. The mellowed stone glowed with the patina of age Bree had noticed in other historic buildings. Long and low, substantial looking, this little village church was no soaring cathedral, but its tall steeple, shaped like the top of a castle tower, had real bells in it!

Against this background, Bree's hopes soared. Perhaps something *would* happen, that this visit might be the catalyst for his coming to faith in Christ.

But—what if they taught something else? What if it was nothing more than a place to fulfill a social obligation?

Did you ever ask him, Tyler? No, she'd never asked. She'd gone to great lengths to tell him what *she* believed, but never tried to find out what he really believed.

"See that tree over there?" he broke into her thoughts, pointing out a tree with one branch jutting a short distance out over the pond. "Nearly did myself in on that one when I was ten!"

She sighed. That wasn't hard to believe. "How?" she asked politely.

"Trying to dive-bomb the bluegills in the pond with stones," he admitted sheepishly. "I leaned out a little

159

too far and fell off the limb. Luckily I missed the water and hit the grass. Heaven help me if I'd gotten wet and muddy as *well* as bruised."

He was chuckling, well into his tale.

"Mother was setting up her lesson for the junior class—she rushed out of the church, stormed across the road, and after a quick estimate of the damages—which turned out to be minimal—hauled me back by the ear." He turned lazy eyes on Bree, watching her face for reaction. "I thought I was in for it. The lesson that morning was on Absalom. Wasn't he the rebellious son of David who got himself stuck in a tree by his hair?"

He looked for confirmation to Bree. She shrugged uncertainly and said, "I think so!"

"Anyway, I thought she was going to have me up before the class as an example of 'Cursed is everyone that hangeth on a tree!'" he finished with a grimace.

Bree burst out laughing at his juxtaposition of the verse with the story.

Not only his mention of the Bible story, but the fact that he even remembered it surprised her. It set her heart racing with anticipation at what might happen that morning. His mother had been a Sunday school teacher. Perhaps, *just* perhaps...better just to trust and see what happened. "It sounds as if you have good memories of the time you spent here as a child," she observed.

"The best," he said quietly. "It was probably the happiest time of my life...." His voice trailed off. "I hated it when we had to leave, when Dad transferred back to Melbourne."

Bree thought she understood that, remembering his bitterness about being sent to his father's old schools in England not long after they returned to Australia.

They didn't have time to say more.

A short, plump, beaming woman in a bright coral-print, two-piece dress grasped the window frame of

160

Neville's door. "Neville! My heavens! What are you doing sitting out *here?* Come in where we can all have a look at you, boy!"

"Mrs. Naismith—" he patted the little hands on the door. "It has been a long time, hasn't it?" He addressed the older woman with warm affection.

She stood back for them to get out of the car and join her, and Neville introduced the two women.

Mrs. Naismith's bright brown eyes flickered over Bree with motherly interest and approval. On her part, Bree was surprised at the strength of the little woman's grasp when they shook hands. She could sense that the old family friend liked her, and it gave her a good feeling about the rest of the morning.

It was impossible not to like Mrs. Naismith, whose twittering chatter, quick crisp movements, and bright snapping eyes reminded Bree of a little finch. The humidity played hob with the older woman's light brown hair, wisps of which curled in little tendrils around her face, defying efforts to confine it in an orderly style.

She shooed them into the church, fussing around them while, one after another, old acquaintances and friends of his family came in, greeted him, and clustered around to catch up on old times. When the bell rang for Sunday school to start, the group broke up. Neville decided he wanted to sit in on the pastor's class in the sanctuary. He guided Bree to one side, a few rows back from the front pew.

Pastor Fay, after introducing Neville warmly and recounting a couple of his childhood escapades, launched into the lesson.

Neville listened politely, but Bree, enchanted with the old-world charm of the building, found her attention wandering. She tried to see everything and appear to be attentive at the same time.

She was used to a simple, modern structure. The arched wooden beams bracing the ceiling like buttresses reminded her of Noah's ark. And the windows were just colored glass simulating stained.

Kirkwood, with the dignity of antiquity, was different. Its windows were the real thing. Rich, vibrant colors depicting scenes from the parables filled the leaded panes of the high, arched windows along each side of the sanctuary. At the front of the church, beneath the point of the roof and above the encompassing dark, carved-wood paneling, a larger rose window faced the congregation. The pipe organ was nestled in a niche to one side of the altar. The choir enclosure, of the same wood paneling, faced the raised pulpit box on the opposite side of the church. Near it, in another alcove that led off to the educational building and social hall, was a baby grand piano.

Bree felt she was being observed in her observations and turned to find Neville's eyes, dancing with amusement, on her.

"It's so beautiful," she exulted in a whisper. "My church looks downright homely by comparison."

"It's all relative," he mused. "Churches reflect the personalities of their congregations. This one was founded by a lot of old-country Scots who felt comfortable with this kind of structure and surroundings And anyway, it's not the church that's important, but what the people in it believe. At least that's what *you* believe, isn't it?"

"Yes, in effect," she nodded. He seemed to remember very well what she believed. But, what did *he* believe? All she knew, from what he'd said Thursday night, was he *once* believed God cared for him.

He seemed different from the man she'd picked up at Metro Monday—more reflective, a little removed. He seemed to be busily studying something in the back of his mind while the rest of him carried out the daily business of his hectic tour.

She hadn't been able to put her finger on it before, but he seemed less restless than when they first met.

The change was most notable Friday. He must have settled something at the filming after his confrontation with Jennifer.

Still, despite what she'd seen and heard last night between them, Gena's predictions gnawed at her heart.

But the fear that grew as the day progressed, her biggest dread, was that he'd go out of her life forever at five o'clock that afternoon without ever telling her he loved her and shared her faith in Christ.

The bell rang again, and the noise of people filing into the sanctuary wafted around them.

"Here, let's move over here." Neville pointed out a pew a few rows back from where they'd sat.

"I take it this is the Ross Memorial Pew," Bree commented as they edged in and sat down. She folded the Xeroxed outline of the Sunday school lesson and tucked it in her Bible.

Neville took the Bible from her and slowly fanned the pages. Bits of paper with verses noted on them, colored satin bookmark mementos of past Easter services, and old church bulletins with still more notations in their margins fluttered in the disturbance.

"Fine way to treat the 'auld buch,' " he muttered with a severe look. Mischief sparkled in his eyes. "Using it for a substitute filing cabinet!" He clucked and grinned.

"I know," she admitted sheepishly. "I've been meaning to clean it out for an age, but I can't bring myself to throw away the notes. You never know when you might need them for something."

"The pack rat's credo if ever I heard it!" he exclaimed with a burst of laughter. As his gaze caressed her face again she blushed with pleasure. He was being so obvious about his interest in her. It would certainly give his old friends ideas about them.

Bree felt suddenly miserable. Where did he stand? *Why* didn't he say something—anything—about his feelings for her, about his faith? Her hopes and apprehensions for the service facing them were almost tangibly painful.

He ran a fingertip over the gold imprint of her name on the green leather cover of her worn Bible. "Brianne Noel?" he raised an eyebrow. "How very pretty—I like that."

She made a wry face. "I guess it beats Desirée LaVerne," she said grudgingly. "Mother was going through a French phase when I was born. Jack was almost 'Jacques' till Dad put his foot down and said he'd be just plain 'John' or nothing."

"Don't you like Brianne, then?" he quizzed in surprise. "I think it's beautiful—fits you perfectly."

"I suppose I should take comfort in the fact that there aren't many others around with the same name," she said.

"Brianne—" his voice, very low, throbbed with emotion.

She looked up quickly, and for a moment all her doubts about him vanished in the blaze of love in his eyes. But he didn't finish his thought. Instead he gripped her hand tightly under the Bible resting between them. Something constrained him. He was deliberately *not* speaking.

"Neville." A woman in a neatly tailored pale blue suit came up behind them, leaning over the high, arched end of the pew to speak. "It's so good to have you with us again!" Bree recognized her as Mrs. Fay, the pastor's wife. "Now, you don't have to do this if you don't want to, but we'd count it an honor if you'd play the offertory."

She didn't press him, only stood politely waiting while he deliberated. Bree was amused to see him blush, however faintly under his tan.

"Mrs. Fay, I'm honored, but I really am out of practice," he demurred, and Bree saw his lack of assurance was genuine.

"My dear," Mrs. Fay patted his shoulder reassuringly, "I remember that your out-of-practice playing was better than some of our *best* efforts!" she reminded gently. "But, as I said, if you'd rather not..."

"You are very good," Bree added her voice to Mrs. Fay's. "I think your friends would enjoy hearing you play—for old time's sake?"

He sighed, "This is the second time you've gotten me involved here. You'll make a believer of me yet!" He rose with a wink, went to the piano in the alcove, and folded back the cover over the keys.

His words were lightly said, but they hit Bree hard. She closed her eyes, feeling tears behind the lids. That he should believe was the thing she wanted most in all the world! Without that, she'd never tell him of her love, no matter how much she wanted to. She would not break her promise. Unless she saw some evidence or he *told* her his faith was in Christ as his Savior, she'd let him walk out of her life at five today and never tell him she loved him.

Not that she had to tell him. She felt so—so—*transparent!* Mrs. Naismith and a short balding man, as thin as she was plump, came up behind her.

"May we join you, dear?" she asked, the brown eyes twinkling hopefully.

"We wouldn't want to impose," Mr. Naismith's quiet voice spoke up behind his wife.

"Surely!" Bree said and started to slide over to make room for them.

"No, you stay right there so Neville won't have to climb over us when he comes back. We'll just squeeze in," Mrs. Naismith said, and they proceeded to sidle around her. "Has that rogue of a boy told you about the scrapes he used to get into here?"

Bree could see she was just dying to share her reminiscences with her. She laughed. Mrs. Naismith was such a pixie.

"Yes, some," she admitted, and she settled back under a torrent of chatter, watching Neville at the piano from the corner of her eye.

The organ music swelled, and the processional began the service. The order of worship was a little different from what she was used to, too, but Mrs. Naismith kept up a running commentary during the Scripture reading and singing.

Neville waited patiently till it was his turn at the piano.

Bree recognized his nervousness by the arpeggios he played softly at first to work himself up to whatever he'd picked. Confidence restored, he struck the first chords, and Mrs. Naismith clapped her hands together in delight.

"Oh!" she sighed. "Do you know what that is?"

Through the masterful embellishments with which he graced it, Bree recognized the tune as "When They Ring Those Golden Bells."

That wasn't what Mrs. Naismith meant, however. "That's the one he won a competition with at the national youth rally just before they moved!" she rhapsodized.

Under his hands the piano became a carillon, pealing the message of the hymn through the vaulted interior of the church. Passing of the collection plates seemed almost secondary to the music.

When he finished, he left the piano nervously and made his way back to them. The suspended silence that followed his playing was relieved by a general sigh of appreciation and several soft "Amens!"

The pastor mounted to the pulpit and began his sermon, but Bree's mind wandered again despite his skilled delivery. Neville fidgeted, scribbling hasty notes on the margin of the bulletin, and making comments or observations to her and the Naismiths the whole time.

Pay attention! Bree wanted to scream at him. *Don't you realize how important this is?* Her anxiety grew as the sermon drew to its conclusion. By the time it was over she felt wrung out.

Stolen glances at Neville's face for any sign of emotion or conviction yielded no hope. He was as blithe as ever. The pastor even gave a rare altar call, and Bree felt her hopes die. As the service ended, she was overwhelmed with disappointment. She retrieved her purse and Bible only half listening as they trailed the Naismiths to the door. Mrs. Naismith turned to lay a hand on her arm.

"That scamp," she chuckled with a nod toward Neville. "He never spends a decent amount of time with us anymore." Her concern was evident as she gazed up into Bree's eyes.

Is it that obvious? Bree thought with alarm, but her straying attention riveted on Mrs. Naismith's next words and Neville's reaction to them: "Don't be too upset, my dear. It won't be for long—"

"Mrs. Naismith!" Neville cut her off with a laugh and a wide-eyed stare. The little woman caught her breath as if she'd almost betrayed a secret and looked embarrassed.

"What I meant to say, you hooligan, is that I know you're leaving this afternoon, but there's no reason Miss Tyler can't join us tonight," Mrs. Naismith recovered admirably.

Neville raised his eyebrows once and patted her arm in affection before turning away again.

Bree wondered, looking at his back, then at Mrs. Naismith. She knew she'd seen a distinct warning pass between them—but about what?

"We're having a little get-together here this evening for the young people and a very good film about John Wycliffe, with refreshments after," Mrs. Naismith continued, righting herself smoothly "Why don't you come and join us?"

Bree sighed. The creeping dread of the afternoon's end drove curiosity from her mind. She shrugged, pulling herself back into the present. Mrs. Naismith awaited an answer.

"I don't know, Mrs. Naismith. It sounds very interesting," she hedged. Any other time her interest in history would win out and she'd go willingly. Now, she wasn't sure what condition she'd be in psychologically after Neville left—or that she'd be fit company for fellow Christians.

"Well, dear," Mrs. Naismith took her hand, patting it.

Bree noticed Neville. He seemed to be listening over his shoulder to their conversation as well as carrying on one of his own.

Mrs. Naismith gazed up with sympathy in her eyes. Bree thought the little woman probably understood her mood too well. "I'll call you this evening, in case you decide you'd like to join us."

She jotted Bree's number down on her bulletin. Neville turned to them again.

"You'll still have the company car till tomorrow, and I can draw a map for you," he offered helpfully, referring with a smile to her tendency to get lost.

"Thanks," Bree said listlessly, "I'll think about it."

"I think you'd enjoy it," Neville prompted. They reached the tall doors at the entrance. "And I think you've passed their inspection—" he teased.

Saying good-bye to his friends, Neville fell in at the end of the line filing out and guided Brianne ahead of him with a hand on her elbow.

"It was a delight to have you with us again." Pastor Fay clapped Neville on the arm as they shook hands. "Don't stay away so long next time! Miss Tyler, we hope you'll worship with us again soon. Mrs. Naismith tells me we have you to thank for returning this errant ram to our flock."

Bree giggled to herself suddenly despite her depression, a picture popping into her mind of sheep horns curling from Neville's wealth of tawny hair.

"I'm going to my office now," Pastor Fay turned

back to Neville. "If you'd care to join me there—"

"Ah, yes, in a minute," Neville cut him off. "I'll take Brianne to the car first and get the book for you."

He said nothing about this unexpected development on the way to the car, and Bree's hopes soared again.

He rummaged through the clutter behind his seat in the car for something and with a triumphant "Aha!" came up with a copy of his book in hand.

"I promised the good reverend an autographed copy of my book," he explained to her curious gaze, and promising to return "in a jif," he jogged back across the road and into the church.

By this time Bree felt like an emotional yo-yo. Hope soared and plummeted in her heart while he was gone.

He returned after ten minutes, chuckling to himself. Bree's heart fell. He was hardly the picture of contrite repentance. Nothing had happened in the pastor's office after all.

In five hours he would walk blithely down the boarding ramp and onto the plane, out of her life.

Chapter Thirteen

On the way back to his house, Neville chatted amicably about anything and everything—perhaps to draw her out of her dejected mood. Bree was sure she'd done a poor job of hiding her disappointment after church. She mentally kicked herself.

Once or twice the incident with Mrs. Naismith crossed her mind. What had she meant, "It won't be for long"?

Neville threw anxious glances her way from time to time during the ride back. Her spiritless participation in the conversation troubled him, but for once he didn't ask what was wrong.

She was grateful for that. It was hard enough facing the inevitable end of their relationship without having to talk about it as well. Besides, she'd be hanged if she'd do that, then end up crying about it in front of him.

He pulled onto a street in downtown Birmingham just down from the theater, slowing as they cruised through the intersection to scan the shops along the right side of the street. A car pulled out of an angled space just ahead of them, and he whipped the Mercedes into the vacated slot.

"Wait here—I'll be right back," he said, and he made a dash for a shop two doors down. Large, knee-high clay pots of brilliant red petunias flanked the red and white striped awning of *Le Petit Chou*. Neville's head just missed the scalloped overhang as he ducked into the shop.

They must have been expecting him, for he emerged hardly five minutes later swinging a large yellow wicker picnic hamper in one hand. He placed it carefully in the back of the Mercedes.

"I'm sure they've done a much better job of making a picnic lunch than I could have," he said with a wink. "I wonder what goodies we'll find?"

Bree wanted to cry in spite of her resolve not to. How could he be so—so heartless? He was acting as if going away this evening were no more than another short separation rather than—she broke off. She just had to brace herself for the end.

He took the scenic route back to the house on the lake, winding through some of the more exclusive surrounding neighborhoods.

Large, imposing colonial homes of stone, red brick, and white siding were interspersed with small, Tudor mansions, set back on rolling hills, removed from the road and prying eyes by long access drives.

More ambitious modern manses, built to blend into their natural surroundings, appeared to merge with the rock falls and stands of trees around them. Through broad expanses of glass meant to remove the unnatural barriers between outdoors and in, Bree caught glimpses of natural wood interiors with sparse, no-nonsense furnishings and shining chrome arc lamps.

Neville turned onto the road that ran by his small lake. The park was already busy with couples and families strolling along the lakeside, feeding the geese and ducks, or just sitting and watching the water. An older man and a boy sat under a poplar spreading its branches over the bank. Fishing poles were stuck in the dirt at their feet. A couple of jays circled, scolding noisily overhead.

Bree's attention was diverted from the scene when they turned into Neville's drive. She was surprised to see the sleek Manta parked up close to the house. Neville pulled up behind it and turned off the engine.

"This place is beginning to look like a used car lot," he complained with a laugh, retrieving the picnic hamper from the back as he got out. "You should have seen the commotion when Bruce dropped it off this morning." He helped her out of the car.

He handed Bree the basket while he shed his tan linen blazer and reached through the open window to lay it across the seat back, then rolled his shirtsleeves to the elbow.

"There!" His tie joined the coat in the car.

"But, other than the fact that Bruce dropped it off, how does the Manta come to be *here?*" she asked.

"Oh, the company thought it would be a nice gesture in view of my father's contribution to its creation....and a nice perk to go with my fee!" he explained.

Taking her arm he headed her gently down the drive toward the road and the park.

"Now, where shall we dine, milady? I leave the choice of a suitably quiet and romantic spot to you." He slipped an arm lightly around her as they walked around the rail fence, stopping at an opening while Bree surveyed the park.

"If you're looking for quiet and romantic I'm afraid you picked the wrong day," she said with a wistful grin. "It looks like today is family day in the park."

"Well, how about over there? That's a little more secluded." He pointed out a copse of young weeping birches at the end of the lake where the greensward widened between the road and the water. Tall, narrow-leaved bushes growing around the four-trunked tree screened the location from the road and from the curious glance of strollers-by.

When they reached the spot, he set the basket down and opened the hinged lid. "Here, love, help me with this!" He lifted a folded white cloth and gave it a shake.

"My word!" Bree laughed in surprise. She grabbed a corner of the linen tablecloth and helped him spread it on the grass. "You've thought of everything!"

"No, apparently not quite everything," he said sadly, settling next to her on the grass. He lifted rueful eyes from an examination of the basket's contents. "I forgot the pickles!"

They settled down to enjoy the meal of cold chicken and beef, with potato salad, fresh fruits and vegetables, and cold rice pudding. Bree marveled at a take-out picnic lunch to order, complete with basket, real linen cloth, and iced tea. It even included a cut crystal decanter and iced tea goblets swathed in big linen napkins.

"You know," he remarked, pouring the amber liquid, ice cubes clinking, into a glass for Bree, "I've yet to decide whether American tea in all its guises is a travesty of a grand old tradition or a hybrid, an entity of its own."

He held the glass up, watching the sunlight pour through and gild it as tiny drops of moisture formed and rolled down its faceted sides. Satisfied with its appearance he handed the glass to Bree and poured one for himself.

She raised her glass for a sip, but he stopped her hand. Holding it lightly he raised his glass to touch hers.

"Brianne," he toasted her quietly, his eyes holding hers, "who's made a dreaded chore into an unforgettable event. I thank Providence for you, Brianne."

It was the closest he'd come to talking about spiritual things that day, Bree thought, but when he leaned over and placed his lips on hers she gave up trying to think at all. His love for her was in his kiss, in his eyes, in his voice—but not in his words.

The glass trembled in her hand and she set it down hastily, wondering why he didn't ask her what was wrong—why he was so distant and distracted. Maybe he was feeling the coming separation as strongly as she and didn't want to talk about it either.

Whatever his feelings he kept them to himself and went on to talk about everything *but* any sort of future they might have after today.

He talked about his plans—and vaguely at that—how grateful and relieved he was that the end of the book promotion was in sight, after this next stop in New York. He looked forward to settling into some semblance of normalcy in a regular profession with regular hours—without ever mentioning what profession.

Each time Bree started to interpose a question about what he planned to do he hurried on to another thought or launched into some anecdote about the tour till her curiosity passed. He was teasing—trying to be funny. He was aware of how she felt. He didn't have to ask what was wrong.

The meal ended all too quickly. Bree glanced at the large gold face of his watch and with a start saw it was two-thirty!

"No cause for alarm," he hastened to assure her when she called it to his attention. He held up a hand. "I have run for planes enough years to know that I'll make this one on time too. I won't spoil your escort record by missing it, my dear." He grinned, placing a fingertip across her lips to silence her protests.

She laughed wanly.

"My *escort* record, as you so wittily put it, begins and ends with you," she reminded him.

His lips twitched with a rejoinder, but he jumped to his feet instead, tossing a handful of food crumbs on the grass nearby. With subdued honks, curious Canadian geese who'd been edging cautiously toward them wagged their tailfeathers and waddled faster to the spot. Neville scooped up glassware and rewrapped silver to chuck it indiscriminantly into the basket.

"Here you go!" he called to the geese, startling them into noisy retreat as Bree helped him to shake out the cloth in their direction. He wadded it into a ball and stuffed it back into the basket. Flipping the lid shut with a bang he picked the basket up, holding it out by the handle to Bree. "Here—you keep it for me—for next time," he said.

She held the handle tightly without realizing it while they retraced their steps to his house. At least he was leaving her something to remember him by.

"We'll go back to your place and pick up the Camaro," he was saying as they entered the foyer of the house, "then drive by the dealership and leave the Mercedes—there'll be a man waiting for it. Gerry will close up the house for me and put the Manta in storage...."

He saw she still hung onto the basket. He took it and set it beside the door.

"You'll need both hands to help me pack," he said.

Casually joking about his messiness, he took her hand and led her to the back bedroom where the big brown case sat open on the king-sized bed, clothes resting haphazardly around it on the quilted rose bedspread.

He chattered endlessly while she handed him shirts, socks, books, ties, and a jewelry box to stow in the half-packed case. He went over to the dark wood triple dresser and opening the top drawer took out a broken picture frame. It looked familiar to Bree. He came back and held it out. Jennifer Thrale's smiling image stared back at her.

"That's extra weight I won't need in my luggage," he said. "Dispose of it as you will."

Bree walked over to the large basket-weave hamper

that served as a wastebasket and dropped in the frame. "A fitting end," Neville observed. He turned away with a smile to finish his packing.

The rental car disposed of, they set out for the airport, Neville driving. He found an empty metered parking place near the main terminal, and Bree held her breath as he backed the Camaro into it.

"*Now's* a fine time to take exception to my driving!" he chided.

"Not at all," she said undaunted. "I admire your ability to park so flamboyantly. Parallel parking is not my long suit."

With such inanities they made their way through the lobby to the departure gate for his flight.

Bree's dread of the parting grew with each step.

They stood a little apart from the rest of the crowd waiting to board. Neville held his suit bag slung over his shoulder, his free hand gripping Bree's.

If you're ever going to tell me, she thought watching the clock tick off the minutes with incredible speed, *now's the time!*

"Brianne," his hand tightened painfully around hers and he turned to look down into her eyes. Behind them his plane nosed to a stop outside. When the boarding announcement blared over the public address system, he shot it a look of annoyance.

Bree cringed inwardly. Their time was gone.

"Brianne," he started again as people jostled past them to the boarding ramp after the steward dropped the guard chain.

"You didn't even give me a copy of your book!" Bree accused, but her voice broke on the words, and she turned hastily away to hide the welling tears.

Neville threw the suit bag down on the flight bag beside him and spun her around to face him.

"Don't ever turn away from me, Brianne, darling," he whispered, wiping the tears from her face with his thumbs. He grabbed her to him in a fierce kiss that ended all too soon, then released her to unzip the flight bag and pull out a copy of his book. "I'm giving this to you on the promise you won't read it till you're at home again. Promise?" He held it just out of her reach.

When she nodded he gave it to her.

"I'll call you when I get to New York," he said, grabbing up his things again, and stumbling backward away from her. He turned then and disappeared down the long tunnel of the boarding ramp.

Bree stood at the glass for a long time, the book clutched to her, oblivious to the last-minute bustling of late arrivals. She peered at the jet with its red, white, and blue stripes, trying to guess which window was his. She wondered if he was looking for her as well.

It won't be for long, Mrs. Naismith's words bobbed to the surface of her mind again. Well, whatever she'd meant, it was too late now.

After a while Bree turned away, remembering an old saying that it was bad luck to watch someone out of sight. She couldn't bear to watch him leave anyway. The roar of the jet's revving engines followed her as she moved with heavy steps back down the empty hall.

"Karen?" The apartment was quiet. Brianne tiptoed in and looked around the living room.

"Karen?" she called again, going down the hall to the bedroom.

Spying a note taped to the mirror in the bathroom, she grumbled, "I don't know why we ever bothered to put a message board in the kitchen!" She read the note: "Spending the night at Mom's—tell 'Digger' good-bye for me! Love, Karen!"

Bree sighed with relief, her body trembling with the effort to maintain her composure on the long ride home again. She moved numbly across the thick carpet, walking out of her shoes as she went and dropping her bag and Neville's book in the chair.

When she reached the sofa, all resistance went out of her, and she collapsed onto it, burying her face in one of Karen's crewel pillows. Against the rough wool of its yarn she abandoned herself to pent-up disappointment and sorrow.

How could she have been so stupid, thinking her little game of using one man to get over the heartbreak of another would be harmless? Neville's leaving hurt more than Spence's ever could have.

She ached all over with the loss.

Bit by bit the storm of tears abated. She prayed, and the peace of knowing she'd done the right thing returned. She'd let Neville go, even though she suspected that at a word from her he would have stayed. But there had to be some other reason he hadn't—his *book!* In her self-pity she'd forgotten all about it.

Bree jumped from the sofa and grabbed the book out of the chair. What had he written in it?

She fumbled with it in her haste to the flyleaf where he'd addressed her in his bold, flowing script.

"My dearest Brianne..." she read. It was his afternoon toast to her, with one crucial exception. The words he hadn't said were there, just above his signature—"I love you."

Bree closed her eyes and leaned back savoring the words.

She sighed. Well, what good did that do? He was gone. And besides, even if he weren't what hope was there? If he hadn't come to faith in Christ, she couldn't respond. She had promised.

Bree recognized that she loved Neville with all her heart—what she'd felt for Spence was a pale shadow by comparison.

Another thought arrested her. She'd never actually asked Neville what he believed. She'd just assumed he didn't believe anything. Her mind seized on evidence and proceeded to pick it apart.

He'd as much as said his mother was a Christian Wednesday night, when he'd told Bree she reminded him of Mrs. Ross. Then at church this morning, Mrs. Naismith didn't seem concerned about the state of his spirit, and she was definitely the type who would be. And what transpired between those two this morning? The question gnawed at the back of Bree's mind.

Stupid! Stupid! Stupid!—The phone broke into her self-flagellation.

Neville had said he'd call when he got to New York. She looked at her watch—too early for that. Blowing her nose hastily into a tissue she picked up the phone.

"Hello?"

"My dear! Did I catch you at a bad time?" Mrs. Naismith's lively voice greeted her.

"No, not at all," Bree apologized, "Just sinuses." Crying *did* block her sinuses!

"Well, you take care of that now," the older woman adjured her. "I just called to remind you of the program tonight...." she sounded anxious. "I do hope you'll come, we're looking forward to seeing you again. Neville thinks so much of you...."

"Thank you Mrs. Naismith—" Bree turned the offer over in her mind. It seemed very important to her caller that she attend tonight. Bree could almost hear her holding her breath for the answer.

Why not? Anything would be better than sitting home waiting for a call that might not come.

"Sure, I'd love to, Mrs. Naismith. The film sounds interesting, and it'll be good to see you again, too." After a torrent of infectious, happy chatter from Mrs. Naismith, Bree went to the bathroom smiling.

She surveyed the storm damage to her eyes and face. A quick wash with cold water and reapplication of makeup repaired things pretty well, but the sinus excuse would have to do for the sniffles.

She changed to the red print dress and matching heels she'd worn Tuesday and carried the blazer in case the night air turned chill.

She reclaimed her purse and Bible from the chair in the living room, and headed out down the stairs to the street door.

Evening breezes disturbed the overhead tree branches, turning the leaves bottom side up to show their silvery undersides.

"Storm coming," she murmured, "or come and gone, in my case." The air did seem cooler. Clouds were blowing in, deepening the shadows in the tree-lined street.

She bent her head to rummage in her bag for the car keys and didn't see a red car pull away from the curb behind her.

With the key in hand, Bree looked up again when she reached the building's side drive to find the red Mercedes blocking her way. The door swung open and Neville peered out to say, "Get in!"

Bree stared uncomprehendingly at him. The parking lot, trees, building spun around her in a dizzying vortex.

"Brianne, get in," he repeated.

Like a sleepwalker Bree moved to the car and lowered herself into the passenger seat. Pieces of conversation dropped into place in her dazed mind. *This* is what Mrs. Naismith meant when she said he wouldn't be gone long—he never actually left!

Disbelief and anger warred in the glance she gave him.

Neville cringed. "I know—" he soothed, "it wasn't really fair, letting you think I left, but I had a reas—Brianne, *wait!*"

He reached to grab her as she swung her feet out of the still open car door and almost ran from the car.

The spike heels of her shoes made a staccato click on the sidewalk as she hurried away from the car, the old trees on the narrow strip of grass between walk and street blurred by angry tears. Bree heard the car door open and slam shut. Then running footsteps followed.

She tried to speed up to get away, but a hand grabbed her arm and spun her around.

"Brianne wait!" Neville's eyes pleaded with her as he spoke. "I don't blame you for being angry, but please listen to me before you run away."

He took both her arms firmly in hand so she couldn't pull away. Bree almost dropped the jacket and books tucked under one arm but Neville released his grip to take them from her.

"Come back to the car with me," he urged softly.

"No! I'd rather—I'd rather walk!" she mumbled, blocking his hand when he attempted to brush away two tears spilling over her lashes onto her dress front.

"Bree, please forgive me," he whispered. "Brianne, I do love you."

Walking slowly, Bree looked up. They were the words she'd wanted so desperately to hear a few hours ago, but hearing them now didn't seem real. Neville pulled her to an unresisting stop. He watched her expression as he tried to explain.

"Bree, I had to be sure of a few things—that I didn't imagine all this, that you—" He stopped, watching her face closely. "Brianne, do you love me?"

"Yes," she stammered after a minute, her anger arrested. "Of course I love you! Why else would I have made such a fool of myself—"

A silly grin spread across his mouth, his eyes caressing her face, and for a moment she thought he intended to haul her into his arms for another of his crushing kisses right there on the street.

Instead he said, "I take nothing for granted. I hoped you—" He looked around uneasily. "Can we go back to the car now?"

She hesitated, still peeved about the deception.

"I'm blocking the drive and the car is still running," Neville pointed out.

"All right," she said, but her eyes told him the explanation had better be good.

He rested an arm lightly around her as he helped her in the car, handing her the books. He got in and took a vacant slot in the building's lot, before turning to explain.

The limited space irritated him, Bree saw as he squirmed around to get comfortable and take her face in his hands. The shock—and joy—of his unexpected appearance made it hard to stay angry with him.

"Why?" she burst out. "Why did you do this to me if you love me?" She sniffled into her soggy tissues while he brushed a wisp of hair out of her face. She made no move to pull away. Neville tipped her face back so she had to look up at him.

"I did it *because* I love you," he said putting a fingertip across her lips when she started to protest. "You had something to prove to yourself—you as much as said so Thursday night when we talked, remember? That's when I first realized how we felt about each other. But if I'd said anything, if I'd told you I loved you before I left—"

She gave him a withering look over the silencing hand.

"—when I *presumably* left."

She acknowledged his correction with an approving nod.

"—if I'd done anything to make you compromise your decision, your promise to God, all your experience with *Kenyon* would have been for nothing. You had to know you could stick to that decision, *and* trust the Lord and His will enough to let me go, not knowing if I'd be back. *You* had to know you could do it."

Neville watched her intently as he spoke. Bree gazed away.

"And you did. You stuck it out. You don't know

183

how I hoped it was really love I saw in your eyes, and not infatuation…"

She turned to him again. He leaned forward to sweep her into his arms, holding her tightly.

"You didn't throw your convictions over for me," he whispered into her hair.

She put her hands on his shoulders in a tentative response, ruminating on his words.

"But why is that so important to you?" she quizzed, still a trace of pique in her voice. "If I remember correctly, you weren't too keen on what I believe, either."

Neville sat back a little to see her eyes.

"Bree, a lot of things can happen to a man to shake a childhood confession of faith," he explained slowly. He turned to focus on her eyes. "My conversion was very blithe—I never questioned belief in Jesus as my Savior after accepting Him when I was eight. My mother was a Sunday school teacher; my father, an elder. It seemed the natural thing to do.

"When I was twelve and faced with the move back to Australia—away from my friends, school, a whole way of life—I prayed very hard that something would happen—that God would keep us here somehow. But He didn't. I know I sound foolish," he sighed, then laughed ruefully. "Everything is clearer in hindsight!"

Bree watched him in wonder for a minute.

"Are you telling me you *are* a Christian?" she asked, afraid to trust her ears.

"The least of the least, and for a very long time," he confessed. "After our talk Thursday, when I realized where our feelings were headed and saw you meant what you said about your promise, I decided it was time to end my private war with the Lord. Oh—" He took a deep breath and exhaled, stretching again, "it wasn't only you. There were other indications that this was the time. The knee, for one. And the end of something I loved—soccer."

He let his hand run caressingly down her arm to her

hand and took it in his again, smiling.

"That's why I went to church this morning and spoke to the pastor afterward," he finished. Taking the crumbling tissues from Bree's fingers, he mopped her face much as he'd done earlier at Metro.

"Bree, I had to find out if you loved me—and the Lord—enough to let me go," he said. "Can you forgive me for the deception?"

Bree's head still swam with the unexpected turn of events. Interpreting her silence as assent he pulled her into his arms and possessed her lips with his. Bree lost track of the time, her anger dissipating as she returned his kiss with equal intensity.

He raised his head finally and pulled her over to rest on his chest, stroking her hair.

" 'Old things are passed away,' as Mum is fond of saying, and I'm going to need your help with the new, Bree. You have to be strong enough to stand up to me when I'm wrong," Neville grimaced in warning and laughed. "But if your temper a few minutes ago is any indication—"

"Why didn't you tell me all this before?" Bree poked his sternum with a finger to emphasize the demand.

"Why didn't you *ask*, dearest?" he quizzed, imprisoning the hand with his and kissing it. "I've been waiting for you to say something since yesterday—maybe even before...."

"But—what about New York?" Bree's mind crashed back to earth and more mundane realities. She sat up abruptly. "You have a book promo tomorrow and a talk show appearance and—"

"Never mind New York or the book. We have more important things to discuss, like a wedding next week!"

"*Next week?*" She fell back against the seat. It may have taken him a while to get around to saying he loved her, but he was wasting no time now.

185

"Too soon? Well..." he relented, his mouth curving into a teasing grin.

"Wait—now just wait a minute, Neville Ross!" She held up a hand. "Give me time to get used to the idea. Everything has been so—"

"Sudden?"

"No," she said slowly. She let her eyes linger over his face, not afraid for him to see into her heart anymore. "It's just now becoming real—that you're here, that you love me, that we share the same Lord. It's almost too good...."

"Is *two* weeks time enough to accept reality?" he teased again. "I'm a very impatient man, Brianne!"

She laughed and flushed in confusion.

"But I just can't leave my job—" She caught herself in midsentence. What job? The assignment at the Tech Center ended with Neville.

"Apart from your attending classes, no one is going anywhere or doing anything for a while. We have the house on the lake to furnish—unless you really do like wide open spaces, which suits me just fine...."

"I thought you were just *borrowing* that." She gave him an accusing look. What else had he been up to without her knowledge?

"Well, I was," he explained sheepishly, "but then I bought it. Remember, I told you the place was special to me?"

She nodded, watching Saturday morning's contentment return to his eyes.

"That's the house we lived in when I was a kid," he said. "I wanted my memories back. Luckily Gerry knew the owners and was able to make all the arrangements for me."

"Was Mrs. Naismith in on—"

He cut her off, chuckling as he pulled her back into his arms.

"Now that was chancy! Trying to keep you from seeing the car at Metro, then rushing back to be here

186

when she called, and *hoping* you'd take the bait—God bless her timing!" He rubbed his chin thoughtfully. "But we pulled it off, Gerry and I—just like old times!"

Bree leaned unresisting on his broad chest, wrapping her arms and her heart around him. After the ordeal of telling him good-bye forever, it was still difficult to believe he was here. The solidity of his form in the circle of her arms made it real at last.

"Now, the only thing holding us up is you." Neville moved to allow for the intrusive presence of the lever between them. "If you think you're quite over your infatuation with Spencer Kenyon—"

"Neville!"

"—do you think you might marry me? At a date and time of your choice, of course," he hastened to add, tweaking a lock of her hair.

She shook her head, laughing. "Do you seriously think you'd get away from me again, after the trick you pulled today? Yes, I'll marry you, and you'll deserve everything you get, too!"

"No," Neville sighed, "I don't, but the Lord is gracious enough to give you to me anyway."

He kissed her again, reluctant to let her go, then settled her back in her seat.

"Buckle up, sweetheart," he said. He stroked Bree's cheek with the back of his hand, then took her hand to rest on his on the shift knob.

"I really do have to go to New York tonight, but when I get back," he scowled at Bree, "I want a definite wedding date from you."

Neville paused, as he maneuvered the car back into traffic.

"Do you think Mrs. Naismith will get to Mum with the news before I do?" he asked. "She'd never forgive me, you know—"

"Who?" Bree teased in a daze of happiness, pinching his hand lightly, "Your Mum or Mrs. Naismith?"